COLOURS IN BLACKNESS

A New Life

Tammy Dunning

COLOURS IN BLACKNESS

ISBN-978-0-9920069-1-4

Special Thanks

My daughter, Mandy Dunning created the cover for this novel. Mandy is an excellent artist with so much talent. Thank you Babygirl! I love you!

My Mother, Sandy, for being the first to read and help edit this book. Your ideas helped make it complete. Thanks Mommy!

The second reader, Cheryl... Even though you were recovering from a major surgery, you still read and corrected a lot of overlooked mistakes. Thank you so much!

The Third reader, Jennifer... She gave the book a teenager's seal of approval which means a lot because she's a big reader. Your help was greatly appreciated. Thanks Darlin'!

CHAPTER

ONE

"Laura? Laura, answer the question please." Mrs. Grant is summoning me. I must have dozed off. This migraine headache is worse than any of the others. The light hurts my eyes, feels like they're actually burning up from the inside.

Two days now. I've had this stupid migraine for two damn days! It's not so bad right now. At least I stopped throwing up. I didn't eat breakfast this morning because I was nauseated and was afraid that I'd puke in class. I'd never live that one down. But now I'm starving.

I'm eighteen years old and I've been getting these ridiculous headaches most of my life or at least as far back as I can remember. But lately, they seem to be getting worse.

"I'm sorry Mrs. Grant, I didn't hear the question." What was I going to say to get me out of this; randomly pick an answer, blurt out something that has no relevance to her question and get laughed at by my fellow classmates? I don't think so.

"I asked you what the capital of Northwest Territories is and what their main industry is. You would have heard me if you weren't napping during the lesson." My teacher is a little snippy today.

Mrs. Grant is a nice teacher, I like her, but she's tough. If you don't pull your own weight, then she'll fail you. But I'm a good student, holding a 3.8 grade point average so teachers don't usually bother with me.

"Oh. Um, well Yellowknife is their capital and I think they mine gold up there." My brain is going to explode. Please don't ask me anything else. I don't want to have to think anymore.

With a smirk on her face, Mrs. Grant adds, "They also mine for coal." She goes on talking about the Northwest Territories but no matter how hard I try to pay attention to her, I just can't focus. I'll probably never go there anyway.

Please let the bell ring so I can get the hell out of here. Wait, no, the bell ringing will be like knives stabbing through my brain. But, at the same time, I know it will get me closer to relief. School will finally be done for the week. TGIF... Huge!

I just want to go home and hide in my room. I'm going to close my curtains and my door; no outside noise, just the sound of my own breathing.

I want to just curl up in my bed with the blanket over my head. Oh it sounds like Heaven right now. I just have to endure the fifteen minute bus ride from Belle River back to Tecumseh.

I live in Tecumseh, Ontario. That's near the southernmost tip of Canada, just across the crick from Detroit, Michigan. That's what a lot of the old timers say, 'just across the crick'.

Tecumseh used to be a small town, according to my Mom who's lived here since she was nine years old. Now it's more like a city even though everyone still calls it a town.

The biggest news of the week is when someone gets their car broken into. Needless to say, it's still safe to walk down the street alone at night.

There's always someone walking their dog here, even in a snowstorm. They just put a goofy sweater on him and sometimes even booties. You can almost see the humiliation on the dogs face as he saunters by.

Living here isn't so bad... boring, definitely. At least we have a huge variety when it comes to the weather. Winter snowstorms where the temp drops to about -20F (-28C) or worse, and summer heat waves of up around 110F (43C) degrees or more. It varies. It's the humidity that'll kill you.

I awaken to the sounds of birds outside my window. Some robins decided to nest in my window box that is usually full of flowers. Of course I couldn't plant flowers after they had created a nest in there. What do I do, throw it over the edge and watch their eggs splatter on the cement below? I'm not that cruel.

Besides, I've enjoyed watching them huddle over the eggs when it was raining. It's gross when they first hatch. They look like ugly little veiny things.

I've been watching them and I never realized how fast they grow from simple little eggs to beautiful robins. They're getting their adult feathers already. They've lost most of their down feathers, which are soft as a cotton ball by the way.

Pretty soon I'll be watching them fly from the nest. Well hopefully they'll fly and not splatter. I think I'd be pretty upset if they fell.

Note to self: Be sure to plant seeds in the box before they come to roost next year so that flowers will grow around the nest. It'll be pretty.

My headache isn't so bad this morning but my eyes are still sensitive to the early afternoon light. Sleeping in until 11:00 is magnificent. There's nothing like knowing that you have absolutely nothing to do so you can sleep for as long as you want.

I finally pull myself out of bed and make my way down to the kitchen. Mom's sitting in the front room watching TV and playing games on her laptop. Probably some dumb 'shoot the bubbles' thing. She seems to like those pointless types of games.

Dad's out in the garage building something. I can hear his table saw wailing away as it chews its way through some poor innocent piece of wood. I wonder what he's making.

His work always looks awesome but I can't figure out why he doesn't just go out and buy the stuff instead of making it himself. That sounds so much easier to me. He says that it gives him a sense of pride for a job well done and that I should try it some time.

Ah, the kitchen… cereal. Lucky Charms are my favorite. I know we have them because I put them away when we sorted the groceries last night.

The cereal tastes so good, the milk is super cold.

Mom comes strolling into the kitchen with her half empty mug heading straight to the coffee pot to get a refill. "Good morning, baby girl! How'd you sleep?"

"I think I might have slipped into a coma not just slept. I had some really bizarre dreams though." I mumbled as I shoved more cereal in my mouth.

It's true… I don't remember having any dreams that actually made any sense. Just flashes of colours with bubbles floating around. I could almost see people and other odd pictures in the bubbles. Nothing made any sense... some really crazy stuff. Nothing like I've ever dreamed before.

"So how's the headache?" Mom sips her coffee and groans because she burnt her lip again. It's a common occurrence.

"Not too bad." A strange feeling waves through my mind almost as though I'm losing control or getting farther away from my physical self. My arms start tingling. The bowl of cereal slips from my grasp and smashes on the floor in what seems like slow motion. I can't move my legs.

Pain... Sheer utter agony. My head is going to explode!

Blackness... I... Can't... See...

Flashes of bright colours flicker and smear together. It's like a kaleidoscope only the multitude of shades blur into each other creating colours that I've never seen before.

I feel like I'm floating, quietly, softly while these colours engulf me. When I move my hand back and forth, the colours blend together leaving a trail of swirls and waves.

I can't help but laugh. This is so amusing. I must be dreaming. My weightlessness is something that I've never felt before. It's almost like I'm swimming through the beautiful hues only I won't drown if I stop moving. I just float in zero gravity amongst blushes of reds, blues, greens, yellows and other colours that, as of yet, have no names. They are unearthly.

A bubble starts to form so far away and slowly coming closer. There's motion inside the bubble like a movie playing. I can't quite make it out.

This is so much like the dream I had last night. Am I dreaming? I wasn't asleep when this started so I must be hallucinating. But why? Maybe it's because of the migraine.

So where am I? What's happening to me? I'm not scared, not panicking. I feel nothing but calmness. No migraine pain.

In the bubble there's an airplane at an airport. Why am I dreaming about a plane, if I am actually even dreaming? If so, this is a really bizarre one. A plane would be the farthest thing from my mind. I've never even been on one.

It's like I've floated right into the bubble. I can see the whole picture now. Everything's so sharp like it's playing in HD or something better. The 747 is driving down the runway getting ready to take off. The wheels lift from the ground and start to fold up so they can hide away into the underbelly.

A blinding flash… Fire in the engines… The plane is going down. I should be horrified but I have no real emotion, I'm numb. Pardon the pun but I feel like my emotions are on autopilot. It is only a dream after all.

In a huge ball of fire, the plane slams into the ground. It rips apart as it skids and drags on the cement. While it's flipping, it's tossing pieces scattering them all over the runway and surrounding field. I look closer at the flying debris. Some of the pieces aren't fragments of the plane, they're people, and some of them are on fire.

In an instant I'm being pulled backwards. Not pulled so much as sucked. As my body fly's backwards through the colours, a trail is left in my wake, swirling with beautiful pastels. The bubble is getting farther and farther away. Again I float in blackness…

I gasp for a breath of air sucking it deeply into my lungs. I open my eyes to see my mom leaning over me with a look of panic on her face. Why am I looking up at the ceiling and lying on the kitchen floor? How the hell did I get here?

"OhmyGod! Laura, are you ok?" Even though she's panicking, my mom is trying to keep her voice as calm as possible. It's a mom thing.

"A plane crashed." I have no idea why that's the first thing that fly's out of my mouth. I should be asking 'what happened' or 'why am I on the floor', things like that.

"What?" Mom's look of panic shifts into a look of utter confusion. She's looking at me like I've lost my mind.

"A plane… crashed. I saw it in the bubble. It was bad, really bad. People… scattered all over the runway. Why did I dream that? Was I dreaming? What happened anyway?" Ok so now I'm starting to panic a little.

"I... I don't know." There's a dumbfounded look on mom's face. "You just dropped your bowl then slumped backwards onto the floor. Your eyes were fluttering and it was like you weren't here. It lasted only about 10 seconds then you woke up. You said you saw a plane crash?" Mom sits back on her legs and shakes her head. "That migraine pain must have really put your brain in a tizzy."

A tizzy? I've grown up hearing that word. "Yeah, the pain got so bad just before everything went black. That's probably why I passed out... pain." I've never passed out before, like ever. It's weird and I don't want it to happen again/ The dreams that go along with it are way too freaky. "I'm ok just let me up."

"Wait!" Mom puts her hand down on my shoulder and looks at my eyes. I mean, she looks 'at' my eyes as if she's studying them. "Your eyes are so red. Why are your eyes like that? They're... well they look like you would if you hadn't slept in a month. Do they hurt?"

I sit up and touch my eyelids. "What? Um, yeah, they hurt a little. They feel heavy, kind of like when I'm super tired. They're red?!"

"You should go lay back down in your room for a bit, just in case it happens again. I'll bring you some more cereal and a cold pack for your eyes. I'll keep checking in on you from time to time. Do you think you should see a doctor?" I shake my head to say no. Mom turns me in the direction of the hallway and gives me a gentle shove towards my room. "A plane? Really?"

I yell down the hall when I'm almost to my room. "No more cereal, I'm kind of nauseated now." How can I eat after watching all those people die? I didn't feel any emotion when I saw it happen but I'm fighting back tears now. It was horrible. If I never see that again it'll be too soon.

The mirror confirms that my eyes are indeed red, very red. I resemble a person with a hangover. I flip on my TV and change my milk soaked pajama pants then flop out on my bed. I can't get the scene to stop playing over and over in my head. Why would I see a plane crash? It's not like I'm fascinated with traumatic events. It just seemed so real. I have to put it out of my mind.

CHAPTER

TWO

6:00 pm? Oh my God, I fell asleep! I bounce up from my bed and strip off my pajamas. I hop across my room because my pants are stuck on my one ankle. I quickly pull on my favorite old purple sweatshirt and my favorite pair of jeans that I threw over my computer chair when I took them off yesterday.

I am supposed to be at Andrea's house right now. I grab my purse, sling it over my shoulder and sprint down the hall, literally.

"Mom, I got to go. I'm supposed to be at Andrea's. We're going out to dinner with the crew. Bye." At this moment I'm thankful that my shoes are already tied loosely so I can just slide my feet into them, not wasting a single moment.

"Wait!" Mom, almost tripping over herself, runs to the door to stop me before I leave. "How are you feeling? Do you really think you should be driving right now? I mean, what if it happens again?"

"No, I'm fine! If I didn't feel good, I wouldn't drive." Actually, I hadn't realized until now that I actually do feel better than I've felt in days. My headache is completely gone. I stop dead in my tracks and look at my mom. "My migraine is gone and I feel amazing… I really do. Don't worry. I love you. Bye."

I pull up to Andrea's house and before I can put the car in park, she's opening the door and hopping in. Its times like these that I wish my car had auto door locks. That would be funny to watch her glare at me through the window especially if it was raining.

Andrea is a little upset that I'm slightly late and she's not shy about letting me know it. "Where have you been? I tried to call you but you didn't answer. I was starting to think that you were avoiding me." She looks over at me probably ready to give me more of an attitude. "Holy Shit! What happened to your eyes?"

I was hoping my reddish eyes weren't as obvious as they were earlier but I'm not that lucky. They must be pretty bad if she can see them even though there's hardly any light in the car. "Um, it's nothing, really. I had a headache incident. I'm fine."

Andrea seems to accept my answer and doesn't press for more information. She just leers at me with a questioning look. "I thought maybe you were trying out a new make-up look and it didn't go well or something. So what, you don't believe in using make-up to cover that up? It's called concealer. You should try it some time." She pauses for a quick moment then changes the subject. "Ok, so why didn't you answer my calls?"

I'm not a big make-up person. Wearing concealer makes me feel like I'm wearing a mask and I don't like it, unless it's Halloween or something. I usually only put on a little mascara and eyeliner if anything. Sometimes I wear tinted lip gloss if my lips are dry.

"Oh yeah, I forgot, my phone is in my purse on vibrate. Sorry. I didn't feel very good today and I fell back to sleep." I really don't want to get into explaining the whole incident while I'm driving. Besides, how can I explain the plane crash dream without sounding like a freak or something?

Andrea doesn't say anything else about it. She just starts rambling on about everything else. That girl can talk. I'm too busy thinking about the plane wreck. I can't get it out of my head. All I have to do is fill in the odd 'really?' or 'oh yeah?' or just nod my head, and she'll keep right on talking.

She is very pretty. Andrea has auburn hair that seems to capture the light as it flows in a soft wave down to her mid back. Her eyes are so deep brown that when lined in black, can make a grown man weak in the knees. She's taller than me by about 4" but most people are taller than me. I'm only 5'2" tall. Yup, I'm short!

Andrea has been my best friend for most of our lives. When a kid kicked me then stole my viewfinder in kindergarten, she gave me her dolly. We've been joined at the hip ever since.

We arrive at the restaurant only about ten minutes late. As soon as Brian notices me walking up to our usual table, he stares with a disgusted look on his face. "What happened to your eyes? You look awful!" His face is crinkled up making him look like he smells something bad. So it is really noticable.

Ronny and Jill both stare at me too with pretty much the same expression. Neither of them says anything but they do whisper amongst themselves. Ronny now looks concerned but Jill's look has changed to her airhead look. That is typically how her face looks anyway.

Nobody has ordered their food yet so we really aren't late. Andrea and I sit down just as the waitress approaches the table. I'm glad I already know what I want. It's the same as always, a burger and fries.

Brian is sitting across the table. He's looking at me with his very sexy little smirk. "I'm sorry that I reacted that way, you don't look that bad. You do look worse than you did earlier today. Man, I thought you were at death's door the way your face was so pale, but now... wow! I wish you didn't have to suffer those damn migraines. At least the blue in your eyes is really pretty surrounded by all that redness." He's trying to suck up to me.

He's trying to make me feel better. Either that or he's desperately trying to make up for being so freaked out in the first place. Brian has never been one for change and my red eyes are definitely a change to how I usually look.

I think Brian is hot. His black hair is cut into short spikes and his eyes are the brightest blue that I have ever seen. He's about 6' tall and built strong. He's into mixed martial arts so he's very athletic and tanned. All the boy has to do is to think about the sun and he tans! Pisses me off, I'm a Casper all the way.

His GPA is 4.0 which is another reason that I really like him. Stupid guys don't do it for me. But his best feature is his lips. They're not big and puffy, nor are they skinny but they sure are soft and warm. I should know, we've made out on a few occasions but it hasn't gone much past the kissing part.

It's not like we're actually dating so nobody knows what to call us. Everyone thinks we should put a title on our relationship. I like to think we are just really good friends with perks.

We've never had sex, although, if I were considering having sex, he'd probably be the one. I don't know, maybe. I'm not sure why I'm holding off on it. I just believe that when I'm ready, I'll know without any doubt.

"Thanks... I think. I slept until 11:00 today. It's been a really long time since I've been able to sleep in that long. After that passing out thing happened, I fell back to sleep for about six more hours. Migraine's gone and I feel great!" I try to slide in the passing out part really quick hoping that nobody will pick up on it so that later on I can still say that indeed I did tell them.

"You passed out? Like on the floor, like seeing little birdies flying around your head, kind of passed out?" Ronny asks me so quickly that each word almost blends into the next. He talks so fast.

Ronny is, well, kind of nerdy. He's about 5'5" and as thin as a rail. He hasn't found his man voice yet and the other guys tease him about it. He's that guy who cares about everyone and would never hurt a fly.

He's had a huge crush on Andrea since the fifth grade. She doesn't even notice him as boyfriend material, which is sad. He'd be good for her. Andrea likes the jocks.

I think her and Ronnie would make a good couple. She could talk continuously and he would never interrupt her. But if he had to, he could get a whole paragraph said before she was finished taking a breath, that way she'd never miss a beat.

"Um, well," how do I explain what happened without sounding crazy? About the plane I mean. "I kind of passed out on the kitchen floor today."

"OhmyGod, Laura! You didn't tell me!" Andrea is concerned but I can tell she's also upset that I didn't tell her first.

"Um, yeah, well, it's no big deal really. The weirdest part is the dream I had when I was 'unconscious'." Everyone's staring at me with wide eyes and hanging open mouths.

I continue on trying to tell the story as short and sweet as possible. "It was nothing like a dream. I saw an airplane crash. People were being thrown from the plane as it flipped and flopped and ripped open. And, it burst into flames on the runway. I wasn't scared. The whole thing was... bizarre."

Everyone is still staring at me. Nobody is saying anything, which is totally out of character for Andrea. I'm so uncomfortable. I hate being the center of attention. Are they waiting for me to say something else? Thankfully the waitress brings our food. Still nobody's talking.

After a few bites, Jill breaks the uncomfortable silence. "Well, thankfully you're ok. The dream was probably some unconscious, subconscious brain, dream thing. Don't worry about it." She's trying to make me feel better. "Now that I'm getting use to your eyes, I think they're pretty." She's always been a little strange.

"Well if it happens again, I really think you should go see your doctor. Maybe you need a CT scan or something. You could have a tumor." Ronny is genuinely concerned but I wish everyone would just drop it.

"A CT Scan... seriously? That's more for bones, I think. If it were a tumor, I think they'd have better luck using an MRI machine." Andrea pulls everyone's attention away from me as she starts into one of her endless speeches. I can finally eat in peace.

My eyes meet Brian's ocean blue eyes, "Are you ok? Like, really ok? That 'dream' must have really freaked you out. I mean, how could it not?"

"No, that's what was strange. At the time, I felt nothing. I wasn't scared while watching the plane crash at all. I was just pushed into the bubble and it played out. I know it's really weird. Eat before your food gets cold." Lucky for me the focus of conversation changes to something else.

By the time I get home the evening news is just ending. My mother is standing in the living room with the remote in her hand and a blank look on her face. She's staring at the muted TV.

"Mom, what's the matter? Are you feeling ok?" I'm half expecting her to fall down. She looks rather weak in the knees. I turn to grab the phone ready to call 911 if she hits the floor and dies or something.

Barely a whisper and without any emotion, my mother says. "A plane crashed. Everyone died."

OhmyGod! I saw it happen... before it happened. Everyone died. They flew out of the plane, I saw it. I can actually feel the blood draining out of my face. "Coincidence… was it the same as my dream? On takeoff, did it roll and burst into flames?"

She turned to look at me and with a single hesitant nod of her head, my whole world changed. Nothing will ever be the same from this moment on.

If I were able to look ahead and see what my future will be like, how things will be so different from what I have planned for my life, to know of the drama and deceit that will occur... I would never believe it.

I run to my room and flick on my TV hoping to catch anything on the news about it. The all-news station will have something about it. I just want to see if there is a video of the crash so I can compare it to what I saw in my dream. Speaking to no one but myself, I utter, "It's just a coincidence, that's all."

The reporter is announcing that 122 people died. Then I see it, a blurry image of a plane skidding out, rolling over, ripping apart and finally, the flaming engine erupting in a huge ball of orange flame. It's playing repetitively like the tape is on a loop. It's exactly what I saw. The only difference is that my view was so much clearer. I could see all the people. In this video I can't.

What's happening to me? Have I somehow become a prophetic person? How?

Usually after people have some odd accident where they bump their heads a certain way they become psychic. At least that's what they claim. But I didn't bump my head. Maybe I did when I fell.

Snapping me out of my fog and making me jump, literally, my phone vibrates and the theme song for Andrea's favorite TV show fills the silence. She must be calling because she's seen the news too.

Before I can even say hello, she starts rambling. "OhmyGod! You must be freakin' out! Holy shit! Did you see the news? They keep showing this plane crash that happened somewhere in the States. Is it like you saw in your vision?" Andrea is obviously as freaked out as I am. She's actually speaking faster than normal, which I didn't think was actually possible.

"Um, yeah… it's exactly how I saw it, identical. It's like that exact tape was playing in my dream, only my view of it was perfectly clear." She must think I'm nuts. I think I've gone nuts.

"Ok, so now you see visions?! OhmyGod… everyone is going to think you are some psychic prophetess girl who can see shit before it occurs. Do you realize that you could have maybe stopped that from happening? I mean, if you knew, like, what the planes number was or whatever. You saw it clearer right, so like, did you see the numbers on the plane?" Andrea said all that without even taking one breath.

"Um, I didn't really think about it at the time." She's right, maybe I could have prevented it somehow. I shut my phone off after talking to Andrea. I just don't feel like talking to anyone else right now.

CHAPTER

THREE

My whole Saturday is spent answering my phone and the text messages that I'm flooded with. Finally around 3:00 in the afternoon, I've had enough and shut off my phone. I swear that everyone in my school knows what happened. Great! They're all going to think I'm some kind of freak.

"Laura, can you come here please?" My mom's familiar voice puts an instant calm over me. She's calling from the kitchen.

Dad's leaning against the counter with his arms crossed over his chest. He isn't smiling… he looks sad.

There's two strange people in our kitchen sitting at the table with half drank cups of coffee's in front of them. Including my mom, all three of them are sitting rather stiff and looking at me. Mom's eyes are red and swollen like she's been crying, a lot.

"What's going on?" I think somebody died.

The woman speaks up first. "Hi, my name is Ginger Adams and this is Bradley Rathem. Would you please come and sit with us? We would like to discuss something with you." Her arm extends to the empty chair that she wishes I'll sit in. What else can I do but oblige her. Curiosity killed the cat as people always say.

Ginger Adams doesn't look like a ginger at all. Her gorgeous hair is long and black as coal, not red like I picture someone who carry's the name Ginger. Her eyes are a deep green and kind. For a middle age woman she's still quite pretty.

She speaks in a soft, gentle tone. "We are here because we've been informed that you had a vision last night which came true shortly after. You must be very confused and scared. I assure you that there is no need to fear your gift. You can learn to control it and be able to use it for good things. You can help people, stop tragedies from happening for instance."

Is she for real? Ok, so like, I just had this 'vision' last night... how could they have possibly found out about this already? Damn, news travels fast in this town. "Ok, um, I'm not really scared, a little confused yeah maybe. Actually, after what you just said, I'm even more confused than I was. Are you here to, like, fix me or something?" Yeah, 'fix me', that sounds stupid, I'm not broken!

The man introduced as Bradley Rathem cuts in with his horribly raspy voice. "No dear, we aren't going to fix you but we can help you learn how to use your gift properly. If you were to come to Salvation Center, we have doctors and teachers that are more than willing to guide you through the learning process. There are other teenagers there that also share your position with having an ability that they've also acquired. You could live in the dorm with other girls and boys that are much like yourself."

Ginger almost cuts him off. "Wouldn't it be great to be around others just like you?" She pauses for a moment. "I'm sure you must know that what happened to you last night will happen again, soon. If you don't learn how to control your gift, it will consume you. Your migraines will continue to worsen. Most of your friends will alienate you. They won't understand about the visions so they will fear you and avoid you. We see it all the time."

"My friends would never alienate me." Would they? No! They wouldn't. "So, this is going to happen again? Why? Is there a pill I can take to make it never happen again? If so, bring it on so I can stay home."

Bradley says, "Laura, it will indeed happen many more times throughout your life. It will never stop. Different visions of course, not that same one. If you don't gain control of them, they will consume you. And if there were a pill to stop the visions, I would consider giving it to you." He smiles at me but it seems like a forced smile, not a real one.

Up until now my Mom has been quiet as a mouse. "I think it's best for you to go to Salvation Center. They can help you get through this... thing. I don't want you to leave home but I want you to learn how to manage this. Please say you'll go." Tears are quietly streaming down her face.

"When do I go? Can I at least bring my stuff?" OhmyGod, I can't believe I'm actually considering this. I don't want this to happen anymore but if I can control it, I can stop it and get back to my life as I know it… right?

"You may bring your things with you. You can have a room to yourself if one's available but some of our students prefer to share a room. It will be your choice." Ginger seems so nice, like a mother almost.

I have a thousand questions. Pick one... "How long do I have to stay there? Will I be able to still come home and visit my friends, on like, weekends or something?" Ok, so that's more than one question.

Bradley's husky voice reminds me of an old cowboy who smokes harsh cigarettes. "Of course you will. Most of our students have to stay on campus until they've acquired the ability to control their gift. But you are allowed to leave after you have total control. With your gift, we've been told that you tend to lose your mental awareness. What would happen if a vision came while you were walking across the street or driving a car? For your safety we prefer you to stay on campus."

Ginger says, "You can come with us now or later tonight. It'd be best if you didn't waste time. Another vision could appear at any moment. The sooner we help you control them, the better. I'm sure you don't want that pain back. We can help with that too. Without us, it will worsen each time a vision is about to appear and the visions will increase in frequency."

How does she know all this? How does she know about the pain? Maybe she's right. Maybe it will be better for me. I should probably go. It's not like I can't leave and come home if I don't like it there, right?

"Why can't my mom or dad drive me in later? It'll give me time to pack and you won't have to sit here and wait for me. I mean, what's the hurry?"

Bradley says, "Well Laura, it's been our experience that the stress and anxieties of a long good-bye tend to bring on another episode. If the child packs quickly and leaves soon afterward, an attack is less likely."

Ginger adds, "Laura, if you forget to pack something your parents can bring it to you another day. If it's important we'll send someone back for it." Her facial expression is so soft and comforting.

I can't believe I'm going to do this, "Ok, yeah. I'll come. Can I bring my cellphone, iPod, laptop and all that stuff? I want to stay in contact with my friends." This is happening so fast. I can't think. Everything that I want to bring, have to bring, is running through my mind at warp speed. I'm bound to forget something.

Raspy voice, "Absolutely. You may bring whatever you'd like. We do have Wi-Fi and cell phones and iPods are permitted during your off time. During learning sessions they are not."

Mom and I start walking to my room, perhaps the last time for a long while. With a cracking voice filled with sadness my mom tries to talk. "I'll help you pack if you'd like. I'll get my suitcases."

She starts to walk through the doorway leading to her bedroom but stops and turns around. "I love you. You know that right? This will be good for you... and when you're in control of all this, you'll be back home. Everything's going to be ok. It's for the better." Tears are still streaming down her cheeks even though she's doing her best impression of a smile.

Who is she trying to convince, me or herself? She's right though, I don't want that pain to come back and not know what to do and worse yet, put my mom through seeing me like that again. When they fix me, I can come home and voila, back to my life, like I didn't skip a beat... right?

Note to self: Study, learn, get better fast!

Dad is helping Mr. Rathem put my bags in the back of their van while Ginger is talking to my mom trying to comfort her with her words. My mom has stops crying. I don't think it's because she wants to, I think she just ran out of tears.

Mr. Rathem and Ms. Adams wait patiently in the van until I kiss and hug my mom. She holds onto me for so long. I know I'm going to miss her and she me. "I'll email you, mom, a lot, every single day if I can. I promise. Dad, I love you."

"Every day if you can. I love you." Mom's voice is so soft.

I squeeze my dad and quickly, before I can change my mind, step up into the van and shut the door.

I hadn't realized it until I buckle my seat belt and we're driving to Salvation Center that my face is drenched with tears.

CHAPTER

FOUR

I've driven by Salvation Center before and seen the building, but right now, standing in front of it; it looks so much bigger than I ever thought it was. I take a deep breath and follow Ginger and Bradley in through the main doors.

"Laura, this is one of our orderlies, Laden Harris. He's been with us for about five years now." Ginger introduces me to one of the hottest guys I have ever seen in my whole life, including in magazines and on television.

I am totally in awe of him. I'm sure my mouth must be hanging open but I just can't help it. I feel like I know him when I look into his eyes. Maybe it just because he's so gorgeous.

Why are we staring at each other? Neither one of us is looking away. He's so... I don't know if there's a word to describe his perfection. Look away Laura, you're acting like an idiotic drooling teenager.

Laden speaks without averting his eyes from mine. "Actually, it's been eight years now and I'm almost graduated from nursing school so I won't be an orderly for much longer." Laden sticks his hand out for me to shake it but all I can picture myself doing is jumping on him, wrapping my legs around him and making out with him.

But I decide to settle with shaking his hand and nodding my head. If I try to speak right now, I'm pretty sure nothing will come out, or I'll say something really stupid. The smartest thing to do is just shut up.

I can't seem to look away from his blue eyes. I'm still staring. He's looked away several times but his gaze keeps coming back to me. Maybe that's just because I'm acting like a hormone crazed teenager in lust. My face must be totally red... I can feel the heat. I blush at even the slightest embarrassment. I hate that about myself.

Laden gives me this hot little sexy crooked smile and raises his eyebrows almost as though he knows what I'm thinking. Yup my face is getting hotter, lovely.

Through a slight laugh, Laden says, "Come on, I'll take you to your room. You're going to have to stay in a single room right now because we just don't have a roommate for you yet. Don't fret, we always have new people coming in or graduated people leaving so unless you like being alone, we'll double you us as soon as we can."

Laden picks up my super heavy, overloaded suitcase like it weighs nothing. He talks while he's leading me down the hallway and around the corner toward the elevators.

His dirty blonde hair hangs in soft careless curls, about 4" long. It lifts and bounces when he spins around flopping casually back into the perfect style for him, messy. I just want to run my fingers through it and tangle the strands in my grasp. Snap out of it!

I open my mouth to speak hoping a voice comes out and that I don't say something dumb. "Um, no, a single room is great. I like being alone." I'm so thankful that I have sound even if it's a little shaky. "What do you mean by graduated? Is this place like high school or something? I was under the impression that it's a hospital."

Stepping into the elevator, Laden pushes the third floor button. "Something like that. You'll find the classes here are definitely not like regular high school. Most of the time classes usually only run for a few hours a day. You'll do one-on-one with counselors too. Each person has their own type of ability and we're here to help you discover everything about yours. Here you're looked at as an individual, that's definitely not like high school, huh? It seems, so far, that nobody's had the exact same talents as you have, at least not quite as accurate. I mean, we've had and still do have Seers but nothing as advanced as you. I suppose you'll be like a test subject, but most of the kids here are and don't seem to mind it. You'll like it here, most do. The only real downfall here is that sometimes there are classes on the weekends too."

"You say that I'm advanced. What do you by that?" I ask the sumptuous man.

"You're not a freak or anything. You just saw every detail exactly as it happened. Most don't... at least not with their first vision." His voice echo's through the elevator and ripples through me.

The doors open and we exit. Laden's leading me to my room. His ass is so tight. Quit looking! I ask, "So how many students live here?"

Laden says, "Well, I think we have about forty kids. Some have gone, moved on to different places. Yeah, I'd say around forty, forty-five. I'm not sure because I only care for the one wing, your wing actually. So I'll get to know you better." He pauses for a moment, stops walking and stares at my face. "Have we met before? You just seem really familiar to me."

He feels it too? Wow, so it isn't just me. "Um, it does feels like that but I'm fairly sure that I'd remember you. I mean, meeting you... remember meeting you." Great Laura, you do sound like a drooling teenager... lovely.

With a gentle smile, he leads me down a hallway that doesn't look anything like a hospital corridor. There's carpet on the floor, nice carpet, plush and soft. The walls are painted in soft beige with really nice pictures hung all over the place. Plants sit on end tables sucking up the rays that float through the windows. It's an environment that's perfect for reading. It's quiet here, like really quiet. It's not overly bright like most hospitals are either.

Note to self: Come here to read or study.

"Once we get you settled, I can take you down to the mess hall for some dinner. I'll introduce you to your neighbor that lives across the hall from you. She's really nice. You probably haven't eaten yet, right?" Laden opens the door to room #312, leans in flips on the light then backs up to allow me to enter first.

"Welcome to your new abode. I think you'll have everything you need here, if not, let me know and I'll do my best to get it for you. You have your own bathroom, huge bonus."

The room is nice, bigger than mine at home. The walls are painted in a soft blue. The bed sits between two nightstands; one has a lock with a key sticking out of it. The white bedspread is thick and fluffy with tiny blue flowers on it. A big flat-screen TV hangs on the wall with shelving on either side of it. There's a tiny little fridge that sits on one of the shelves.

Against the wall opposite my new bed sits a tall dresser. A walk-in closet is right at the entrance, hidden behind two sliding mirror doors that go from the floor to the ceiling.

The bathroom is a nice size and it has everything I'll need; a sink and vanity with another huge mirror, a toilet obviously, a big stand-up shower with etched glass doors that would hide my privates if anyone were to walk in. I hope that never happens. I shudder at the thought. Ok, I think I might like it here after all.

Laden opens the curtains to a huge window so I walk over to look out. It overlooks an amazing courtyard filled with flowers and shrubs. People are sitting outside on cement benches with cement tables. The grass is greener than any grass I've ever seen around here, especially this time of the year, fall. Usually it's brown and has not yet recovered from the blazing heat of the summer. All of this is surrounded by one building with huge windows like mine, but they reflect on the outside like mirrors do.

"Ok, I'll just leave your suitcase here on your bed and you can unpack after we get something in your belly." I'd love it if he could put the suitcase on the floor and put me on the bed, with him! Snap out of it! Great, I'm blushing again.

We arrive at what appears to be more like a restaurant than a mess hall. Laden shows me where I go to get my food and tells me the best thing ever; the food is free here! I love food.

Note to self: Don't pig out, stay healthy!

What a spread. It's an Italian theme tonight and there's so much pasta. I really think that I will like it here. Laden also tells me that they switch it up, every night there's a different theme. My stomach is growling now.

After I fill a plate with food and grab a papaya juice, Laden leads me over to a table of kids about my age. "Hello everyone, I'd like to introduce you to our newest addition, Laura

Sadie. Laura, this is Tara Remi, Reilly Jarlen, Todd Dunkin, Jessy Bell and Sherri Harper. Tara, Laura is your new neighbor right across the hall from you. Maybe you could help her get settled in."

"Yeah, no problem. Nice to meet you Laura. Come sit. By looking at your eyes, I can tell that you're a Seer. All new Seers come in with red eyes. You'll learn how to control that." Tara points to the empty chair next to hers and she puts her hand out for me to shake it. I put my plate down and shake her hand, then Reilly's, Todd's and Jessy's. I put my hand out to shake Sherri's but strangely she grabs my hand and shakes it quickly. Her hand feels like its vibrating or something. I jump and let go.

Jessy smiles and giggles, "Got you, did she? Don't worry about it. Sherri's ability is to read people when she touches them. She can see what you're thinking and feeling, and your history. She tries to avoid touching people as much as possible because she hasn't learned how to shut her ability off yet."

Note to self: Don't touch Sherri.

Sherri is really pretty. Long dark brown hair that has an almost out of control curl to it, but it suits her. Her eyes look black as oil. Her lips are full, pouty, and she has the smoothest, silkiest skin. She has an average build, perhaps athletic.

"Sorry, I'm sort of new here too and she's right, I can't shut it off. I didn't mean to read you but since I did, you don't have to fear us. We're the best group of kids here when it comes to being friendly. Well most of us, Reilly's not always friendly." Sherri smirks over at Reilly.

The best way to describe Reilly is to say he's pretty much an average looking guy. His hair is dark brown along with his eyes. He doesn't look to be too tall, maybe 5'7" and kind of chubby.

Reilly leers at Sherri, looks up at me and smiles cocky-like. "It's nice to meet you." And immediately goes right back to eating.

Note to self: Stay out of Reilly's way.

"Reilly's a Controller which just means that he can put ideas into your head without you even knowing it. Like, he can make you throw your fork at Sherri if he wanted to. But he won't, right Reilly?!" Tara looks over at Reilly who doesn't even bother to look up from his spaghetti.

Tara continues the in-depth introductions. "Todd can control your body temperature, your moods, that kind of stuff. He's a Controller as well, but his ability is a little different from Reilly's."

Suddenly my body gets really hot. I look at Todd. He's smiling a huge smile and winks at me.

I ask Todd, "Is that you doing that?"

He replies, "It's all me babe." He must be taking back the hot feeling because I'm getting back to normal.

Todd looks like he stepped out of a magazine. Black hair cut short, stunning blue eyes, about 5'10", thin. Oh and did I mention really gorgeous?!

Note to self: He's hot, way out of my league.

"Watch out for Todd. Don't trust your emotions when you're around him, he likes to play with them. We're not supposed to use our talents on each other but he does it all the time. If he uses them on you just tell me and I'll deal with it." Tara's giving me fair warning. She rolls her eyes.

Jessy waves his arm in the air and says, "I'm a Holder. Basically I hold time. Actually I speed up so time seems to hold still. At least that's what we think. They're still studying me. But that's basically why I'm here."

Jessy seems normal. He looks like a surfer kid with his blonde hair and green eyes that look like they're always laughing. He's built average, athletic, about 6' tall.

"I'm a Drifter which simply means that I can totally leave my body and go places. It's kind of fun." Tara takes a bite of her garlic bread and goes on to explain. "The farthest I've gone was about a kilometer. I don't like to go that far because my spirit is pulled all that way back into my body so fast that I get a vertigo sensation and usually puke. But that's not really dinner conversation is it?"

Pulling apart his bun, Todd asks me, "So what is it that you're gifted with exactly?"

Everyone stops eating and looks at me. They sure are a curious bunch. I can feel my face getting red again.

I'm not sure how to explain it. "Um, well, I had a migraine and I saw something, like a movie in my head and then it came true. I don't know if you know anything about the plane crash that recently occurred, but I saw it before it happened. The fuzzy video shown on the news is exactly how I saw it happen only my version of it was crystal clear. It's only happened once." I feel so out of place.

Sherri shudders and says, "Yeah, I saw it when I touched you. Definitely a graphic scene that I hope to never see again." She looks up at me and smiles. "But you're good people, I saw that too."

Everybody goes on chatting about me, my vision and the crash itself. I'm just glad the attention is more or less off me and I can eat in peace.

CHAPTER

FIVE

I actually had a great night's sleep. This bed has a super comfy pillow top mattress. And I had no migraine what-so-ever. It can't get any better than that. Except that I already miss my mom and dad.

After the fog of sleep dissipates, I try to remember what woke me up in the first place. I think that someone knocked at my door. I flip back my covers, hop out of bed and walk over to open the door.

Nobody's here. I look both ways down the hall and still, nobody. Just then Tara, from across the hall, opens her door.

"G'morning." She says through a yawn. "How'd you sleep?" She stretches her arms up high over her head then lets them fall limply down to her sides.

"Awesome, actually. These beds must have magical powers because for the first time in three days, I didn't have any pain in my head when I woke up." I pause for a second then ask her, "Do you know if someone knocked on my door or did I just imagine that."

"Oh, every morning around 7:00 someone will knock at your door, just two knocks, to wake you up in case you're not up already. You'll get used to it. Sometimes they knock to let you know you have paperwork or mail or something. They put it in your slot beside your door. You have something there. It's probably your schedule if you didn't get one already." Tara, still yawning and stretching, waves to me. "I'll come pick you up in an hour and we can go get some breakfast."

I nod to her, bring my paperwork into my room, take an orange juice from my little fridge and sit back down on my bed. It's my schedule, a list of the 'house rules of conduct' and a map of the school. Well, I have English, Human Behavioral Science, Concentration class... wait a minute, what the hell is Concentration Class? "What the hell did I get myself into?" I leave the papers on my bed and head to my bathroom for a shower. I'll read the rest of the schedule later.

The breakfast spread is amazing. They even have my favorite cereal, Lucky Charms, in a cute little box. We sit at the same table with the same people that I met last night. Not much conversation to be had this morning.

Everyone sleepily stares down at their food, yawning and rubbing their eyes through most of the meal. Once in a while someone will look up and smile at me if we meet eyes.

Tara reads over my schedule and shows me on the map where all the rooms are that I have to go to. She even explains to me that basically Concentration Class is about how to control our emotions and our anxiety levels. Ok, so now I know, sort of.

She says that no matter what grade you were in at your regular high school, it doesn't change what we have to learn here. Basically since I was in grade 12 in my high school, I still have to start out as a beginner in most of my studies.

Tara also tells me that there aren't a lot of kids here so they put beginner kids in with the experienced kids but they study their subject at different levels.

We eat breakfast while I'm bombarded with questions. How I actually finished my food, amazes me. We empty our trays and everyone splits up to go their own ways. Sherri has the same class as me so she walks me there.

A headache is starting up quickly worsening. By the time we get to the classroom it's a full blown migraine. I hope it goes away just as fast as it came. I've been told that stress brings them on and God knows that I've been a little stressed these last few days.

I sit beside Sherri and she hands me a textbook. "Here you go. You're going to need this."

"Thank you." The pain in my head is increasing at a faster pace than it ever has before and so much more intense. It seems like the lights are getting brighter in here. The teacher starts talking and writing something on the blackboard but I can't even focus on what she's saying let alone writing.

Sherri whispers to me but it sounds like screaming. "You don't look good. I'm going to touch you and read you. Is that ok?"

All I can do is nod my head and even that is outrageously painful. I can feel her hand on my arm, tingly and warm, vibrating. Sherri's hand leaves my arm. I hear her chair scrape on the floor and that causes me more agony.

Hands, vibrating hands pull on my shirt and help lift me out of my chair. Sherri is guiding me out the backdoor of the classroom. "You're going to be alright. I'm taking you to see Nurse Carol. She'll give you something to stop that migraine. I can't believe anyone can have that much pain. I felt it when I touched you."

That's when it happens. I feel the same as I imagine getting hit by lightning would feel. Sheer, utter pain! My body stiffens.

Blackness… I'm floating through the blackness, the nothingness. Then colours… spiraling… swirling magnificent shades coming towards me blending into the blackness until it takes over and the colours are all I can see. Through the vibrant shades, I see it, the bubble. I really don't want to see what's in the bubble but I can't look away. It's getting closer. Then I see clear as a bell. It looks like a mall. I'm pulled into the bubble.

I stand overlooking a food court. There are a lot of people here. The floor seems to quiver slightly. The ceiling starts to crack and shake. Dust falls and people start running, scattering in a panic. The ceiling is falling down landing on some of the people, squashing them. Then it's just a cloud of dust and I am being sucked backwards through the colours, through the blackness.

I gasp for air. It takes me a moment to realize that I am lying on the hallway floor outside of the classroom on top of Sherri's leg. A group of kids are all around, staring.

As I sit up, I shuffle off of Sherri's leg and turn to apologize but what I see in her face is utter terror. Tears are pouring down her cheeks dripping off her chin onto her blue shirt. She must have seen what I saw only she doesn't have the emotion blocker that I seem to have during a vision. She may never get over this. I feel awful.

Well, the good news is that my migraine is gone… not even a mild headache... nothing.

In the midst of sobs, she yells, "We have to warn someone. We have to stop it. Where is this going to happen... when??" It's so obvious Sherri is just as freaked out as I am, maybe more so.

A nurse comes and checks me out to see if I'm able to walk on my own. Of which I am. The two of us head down to see Doc Turner.

"It's nice to see you again Laura. However, your gift seems to be coming to you at a very fast pace, doesn't it." I nod at the big man in the white jacket. A man I've known my whole life. He's my pediatrician, Doc Turner. He has been treating me since the moment I was born.

He's a very gentle man, soft spoken. Even now at my age of 18, he still wants to be my doctor. Pediatricians rarely ever treat adults and an 18 year old is considered an adult. He still gives me a sucker after every visit. His hair, once brown, is now almost all grey, well, whatever hair he has left on his head. I think when it fell out of his scalp it re-rooted in his ears and nose.

He's been increasingly becoming more and more portly throughout the years. Him being just under 6' tall and 250+ lbs., he's large and in charge, as they say. His belly leads him around and I think he might just be ready to give birth to a baby elephant any day now.

"How are the migraines my dear?" His short, sausage like fingers are pressing at different spots on my head and then down to the glands in my neck. "Does this hurt?"

"No, that doesn't hurt. Migraines are getting worse. I see things when I have them now. Nobody can tell me why. Will you tell me anything?" I try to speak normally but it's hard when someone is flashing a tiny, really bright pen light in and out of your line of vision. Now I have red spots everywhere I look, great.

Doc Turner comes at me with one of those huge Popsicle sticks. "Stick out your tongue and say ah." I comply and hope that my breath isn't horrible. "Well my dear, we really can't say why these afflictions are developing in some teens. Theory is that it's something environmental, but who could say for sure? That's why we have rounded most of you up and brought you to one place. Hopefully we will be able to study your genetics, past histories and behaviors and see if there is a common link to explain everything." He smiles at me with his pudgy face.

"Have you found out anything? No matter what it is, like, if I never, ever have another bite of ice cream than this will never happen again. Please tell me, no matter how stupid it sounds." I am so totally serious. Please let it be that easy.

Doc Turner gives a whole body chuckle, "No, my dear Laura, it is not that simple. We haven't found any common food link. But you don't worry yourself about those issues. Leave it to the professionals. We would all like it if you would just go to your classes and learn how to ease yourself into the controlling and managing portion of your gift and let us worry about the rest."

"A gift? Yeah, I'd like to exchange it." I still hope it's something simple and that they'll figure it out soon. The doc helps me off the table and ushers me out the door but stops to hand me a sucker and a slip of paper.

"Take this to Nurse Lorraine. She's the head nurse for your floor and she'll fill this for you. It's a prescription for a mild sedative to help you. Put one drop under your tongue as soon as you feel the migraine coming on and it'll ease you through the pain process. If you ever have anything that you think might help in our discovery process, write it down and when we meet each week for your evaluation, we can go over it. Is there anything else I can help you with today?"

I shake my head no and try to read the messy writing on the paper. I'll never understand how a pharmacist can ever fill a prescription correctly.

I have about an hour to go to my room and take a nap before dinner. I could really use a nap. Migraines tend to exhaust me quicker than running a marathon would. Not that I'd ever run a marathon, too much work for me. But before I even reach my door, I see a yellow sticky note stuck to it. I walk over and peel it off. 'Please come to room #15 as soon as you get this. Thanks, Arianna.'

I put my books in my room, give the prescription to Nurse Lorraine, then head down to meet this Arianna person, whoever she is. At least on my map it shows that her room is close to the mess hall. I hope this doesn't take too long, I'm starving. So much for my nap!

CHAPTER

SIX

I arrive at door #15. The sign on the door reads 'Arianna Phillips Vision Analyst'. My knock on the door is answered by a quick, "Come on in." The voice is so soft and definitely girlie.

"Hi, I'm Laura Sadie." I hold up the sticky note. "This was stuck to my door."

This room is definitely that of a woman's design, a very feminine woman. It has big puffy couches with soft fluffy pillows and multiple photos of a fat white cat framed in silver placed aimlessly all over the shelves. Dusty-rose coloured carpeting and white wallpaper with thousands of tiny pink flowers all over it. Dear God it looks like a barbie-doll threw up in here!

I sit down on her light blue sofa. She slides gracefully out from behind her desk and shakes my hand.

Best way to describe Arianna is that this room does suit her. She looks like a Barbie-doll. She's young, probably only about 23 years old. Her hair is platinum blonde, long down to her waist and straight as an arrow. Her eyes are sky blue and her skin is perfect. She definitely should be modeling, not dealing with a bunch of kids all day long. She could totally be rich and famous.

"Hi Laura, I'm Arianna. It's very nice to meet you. My job here is to help you decipher any messages that come to you through your visions. I'm called a Vision Analyst." She sits about a meter away from me in a puffy purple chair and immediately kicks off her shoes and folds her legs up under her butt. "I don't really do anything fancy, I'm the person that you can tell all of your visions that you see through a migraine and also the dreams that you have at night when you're asleep. You can always tell them to me, even if they're sexual dreams. 'If it stands out, dish it out' I always say. I will not judge you in any way, shape or form. Dreams can sometimes tell us information that we need to help figure things out. The dream, slash visions, also help to determine where you're at in your understanding process to learning your craft."

Arianna puts a clipboard on her thigh and tells me, "I'm going to write down key points of your last vision. It will help us to put all of the pieces together and try to figure stuff out. Ok, all I want you to do is first, take a deep breath, then I'd like you to tell me all the details of your dream. No matter how tiny or insignificant you think it is. If something was shown to you then it must be relevant enough for your mind to make it a point for you to see it. So start from the beginning."

She seems like a person I can really let my guard down with even though I don't normally like prissy type females. She isn't snooty like most primpy girls are. She seems casual, caring, like a big sister. At least, that's how I imagine a big sister to be. I have no siblings.

I fill her in step by step with everything that I saw in my vision. A few other details stand out that I hadn't even realized that I'd even seen. Like, there was a shoe store on the left and a jewelry store right next to it. I could see a Taco stand, juice store and cinnamon bun bakery straight ahead of me. Things I hadn't even thought about during the vision.

"I'm going to do some research about different malls and see if one matches all your details. If I find something, I'll be sure to call you back down so we can discuss it." Arianna shakes my hand again and I leave her office.

Note to self: Arianna seems to be pretty cool.

On my way to the mess hall, I run into Laden, the extremely hot, delicious orderly who walked me to my room for the first time. My stomach flutters and flips, not because I'm hungry, but because he is the sexiest man I have ever met. Even his walk, or should I say swagger, is mesmerizing.

"Hi, it's nice to see you again." My voice actually comes out and sounds normal, no stuttering or cracking, which is surprising to me. Laden is so breathtakingly gorgeous.

"Well hello there, Missy. How are you adjusting?" Laden's voice is so smooth. I lose myself in a stare watching his plump, kissable lips form his words. I just want to touch my lips to his. I bet they'd be soft and warm. His mouth looks so inviting.

Suddenly I realize that he's stopped talking and is looking at me, waiting for me to respond. I must look like a tomato face because I can feel the blood rush to my skin. "Great! I'm... great. The kids you introduced me to are really nice. Tara's been helping me out with a lot, you know, showing me around and stuff."

"That's awesome. Yeah, they're great kids. So I hear you had a vision earlier. Was it worse than the first one that you had? I mean pain wise. I'm not going to ask you about the tragedy that played out. I just want to know if you're ok." Laden seems truly concerned. Ok so now I really, really like him. He's eye-candy and he's also very caring?! Way too good to be true.

"It was worse pain, at least at first but when Sherri touched me, I don't know. I think she absorbed some of it somehow. She felt and saw everything I went through. I feel really bad about that." I pause and can't help but giggle, "She doesn't ever want to touch me again."

Laden's eyes travel down to my chest then slowly back up to my eyes. He speaks softly in barely a whisper, "That would be a pity." He reaches his hand out and strokes the length of my arm from the top down to my elbow. "I'll touch you anytime."

I can't breathe, I actually think my body forgets how to… until I gasp, not a nonchalant gasp either. I can't speak. All I can do is smile and nod, like a star struck teenager. Was he hitting on me? No way, he's way out of my league! My mind is running away with things again.

"If you're heading to the mess hall, I'd love to escort you. I'm on my way there as well." Laden wraps his arm around my shoulders, pulling me to his side and starts walking towards the mess hall. Thankfully my legs actually work.

"I haven't seen you around. Where have you been hiding?" What I want to say is something like 'please come around all the time so that I can ogle you'. But I am just lucky enough to be able to say what I did without it coming out all jumbled.

Laden takes his arm from my shoulder so he can open the door to the mess hall. At first he doesn't answer my question. He waits until we are through the door and heading towards the kitchen to answer me. "I was needed in a different area of the hospital. It's restricted from the students." He starts to walk away from me then turns and says, "I'll stop in and check on you when I can, maybe later tonight. Is that ok?"

"Yeah… I'd like that." I will really, really like that. I'd love it if he came into my room and wrapped his arms around me while he kissed me passionately...

My stomach flutters and my face turns red again. I've never gone past the kissing part, a little touching maybe, but I've never gone all the way or even anywhere close to it. What if he thinks that I will? Maybe he thinks I'm one of those kind of girls that will even if they don't really know the guy. I really hope not.

The mess hall is filled with people, kids and adults too. I grab a diet soda and a package of two chocolate chip cookies then head to the usual table where Tara and the others are sitting. All of them are staring intently at me as I sit down.

"I'm fine, everything's fine, nothing to worry about." I speak very quickly hoping that it will stop the massive flood of questions that I know are going to be pouring out at me.

"Don't worry about it. I filled everyone in already. They know everything." Sherri speaks in a soft, sad voice. I can't help but feel really bad. After all, it was through me that she saw all that chaos and death.

"Sherri, I'm really sorry you had to see and feel all of that." What can I do to take it all away? I would if I could. I slide the cookies over to her. "Peace offering."

"It wasn't your fault Laura. You didn't do anything wrong." She picks up the cookies. "Peace offering accepted. The combination of the intense pain and the awful vision that followed… was horrible. I've never felt pain like that in my life and hope never to again. You didn't lie when you said that your visions are crystal clear, like in high definition or 3D or something even better. Please remind me never to touch you again when you're having one of those things. I don't ever want to witness anything like that again."

Todd says to Sherri, "I wish I was there. Maybe I could have calmed you both so that it wouldn't have been so bad. Hopefully I'll be around next time. I'm sorry that you both had to go through that." Sometimes Todd can be really nice.

Sherri says, "Thanks Todd but I do not plan on being anywhere around Laura when she does that vision thing and if I am, I'm running the other way. There is no way that I'm going to even risk the chance of her falling on me again." She shakes her head and waves her hand in front of her face before she picks up her milk and takes a drink. She continues, "Laura, did you have a chat with Arianna? When I saw her, I described as much of the details as I could remember no matter how screwed up it seemed. Maybe she can figure it all out because I'm just washing my hands of it. I can't deal with it." Sherri looks really tired. I probably do too.

"Sorry, again. I did talk to Arianna. Does anyone know if she's ever been able to stop a tragedy from happening after someone sees a vision of it?"

Jessy swallows his bite of burrito before he says, "Nobody's ever had visions like you before. At least not that we know of." Everyone stops eating and looks up at Jessy. He looks from one face to another. "What?"

"That's not totally true." Tara looks sad. "What about Mabel Whitson? She had horrible visions too before her..." Tara stops talking and drops her eyes down. I don't think she purposely meant to stop talking, like there's a big secret or something, I think she got a lump in her throat and actually couldn't finish her sentence.

When nobody speaks up, I have to. "Before she what?"

Reilly lifts his head from his plate. With an obvious 'it-doesn't-bother-me-anymore' expression on his face, even though I can tell he's hurting, he says, "Before she slipped into a coma. She wouldn't take the medicine that Doc Turner gave her for the migraine pain. She said that there was some kind of conspiracy or something; that if she took it she wouldn't see all the details of the visions. She believed that what she saw would lead us to all the answers. So when she had one of her intense visions..." He can't finish his thought because his voice is starting to fail him just like Tara's failed her.

Todd clears his throat and swallows down his own lump. "The pain must have been too severe for her to handle. She slipped away, into a coma. We haven't seen her since."

Tara tries to draw everyone's attention away from Reilly by explaining what he can't. "Reilly was really close to Mabel. They were dating." She's whispering as if she's trying to speak low enough that it won't hurt Reilly's feelings. She looks down at the table when she speaks. "Mabel kept telling us that the medicine was bad. She said that everyone, meaning the doctors and nurses, are making us have these inflictions and that we are some kind of experiment to benefit some rich guy or something. I think she should have just taken the medication. We all have to take something sometimes. It helps."

Todd whispers as though he doesn't want anyone to hear him. His eyes scan the room. "There is some weird shit that happens around here though. At times, a member of the staff will say something that doesn't quite make sense. They'll immediately try to correct themselves, like we won't notice the slip. Makes you think, doesn't it? Maybe Mabel was onto something."

Everybody goes back to eating and doesn't say another word about it. They don't say anything at all for what seems like an hour but is more like ten minutes. They're all lost in thought. I wish I had some of Sherri's talent so I could read their minds, especially Todd's. I'm curious as to what he means by 'weird shit' but I decide to let it rest for now and ask again at another time.

After dinner we all head back to our own rooms to do our homework or whatever. We'll meet up at Sherri's room later on. From there, we'll figure out what to do with the rest of our evening.

As for me, I just want to get back to my room and call my mom. I really need to hear an old familiar voice. She's always been there for me and I doubt my being here could ever change that. At least, I hope not. It does put somewhat of a strain on us though. I'm used to going home every night and having my mom there whenever I want or need her. The distance is hard. Soon enough I'd have to move away for college or whatever anyway. I was just hoping that I'd have more time.

At the end of the day, I'm alone.

CHAPTER

SEVEN

I was right about talking to my mom. It did make me feel better. I didn't realize just how much I miss her until I was talking to her. I told her all about my vision and how Sherri felt it too. Then I told her all about my new friends and their 'afflictions' and about the medicine Doc Turner suggests that I take.

Before I know it the time has flown by. After hanging up, I barely have enough time to change into my jogging pants, a huge t-shirt and tie my hair up into a ponytail when I hear a knock on my door.

Tara's here to collect me so she can show me where Sherri's room is. Tara has on a pair of pajama pants with little pink and purple hearts all over them and a massive purple t-shirt on that goes down to her knees and has 'Don't wake a sleeping bear' written on the front of it. Good to know that I'm not under-dressed.

Sherri's room is one floor up from mine, almost directly over where my room is. She's in room #415. Tara just opens the door and walks right in like it's her room. Everyone is already there waiting for us.

Todd is dressed in green and blue checkered pajama pants, a white t-shirt and black housecoat. He's flopped on Sherri's bed with her pillow wedged under his head. "We were thinking that we'd head back down to the mess hall, get ourselves snacks. I prefer a bag of popcorn and a huge bottle of pop. Then we can go to my room, turn the lights out and watch a movie. It's your choice tonight sweetheart, since you're the new girl." Todd raises and lowers his eyebrows and grins at me in a 'come-kiss-me' way.

I look away from Todd quickly. "Um, yeah... about that, I don't want to pick the movie. I don't know what everyone likes." I really don't want to pick the wrong movie and have everyone hate my choice.

"Well, Todd has a vast assortment of movies to choose from. We watch all types of movies so any choice you make will be a good one." Jessy smiles at me. "I think I'm going to have a banana split with caramel ice cream and chocolate syrup, topped with whipped cream. Sherri, what are you craving?"

Sherri stares off into space for a minute before she answers. "I think I'm going to go for a bowl of pudding with a fruit topping... and whipped cream, of course."

Reilly, who looks much happier than he did earlier, pipes up next. "You always have something with fruit on it. Why don't you try to shake it up a little? Maybe go with what I'm going to have, jelly beans and hot chocolate. Not blended together. Laura, what's your favorite thing to treat yourself with?"

For a moment I think about what the two would taste like if they were melted together. "I'm definitely not going to melt jelly beans in hot chocolate either. Well, I like salt and vinegar chips. Do they have chips?"

Tara throws her arm around my shoulder and gives me a little squeeze. "I'm right there with ya sister, chips are always my thing... barbecue baby! Mm mm mmm."

Jessy stands up from where he's sitting on the floor. "Are we ready to go then, 'cause I'm getting hungry talking about all this food?"

Everyone stands up all at once with nods and 'yups'. We file out the door and down to the mess hall where we pick through all the junk food then scurry up to Todd's room. His room is also on the fourth floor, room #425.

His room is bigger than our rooms are, makes me wonder how he got so lucky. He has a queen size bed instead of a double like us. On his floor are four beanbag chairs. The television he has is a huge flat screen probably a 60" and it hangs on his wall. His bathroom has an oval two-person tub and a shower stall.

Note to self: Find the list so I can put my name on for a room like this!

Todd and Sherri flop on the bed and shove pillows under themselves to prop up. The rest of us pick a beanbag chair and flop into it. Jessy puts a tiny little table between us so that we can put our drinks on. We don't want to set them on the carpet and risk tipping them over.

Jessy flops into the beanbag chair next to me. "The movies are on that wall. Take your time and pick whatever you'd like to watch." His smile is nice, warm, comforting. He's really trying to put me at ease about what movie to pick.

I struggle trying to get out of the beanbag chair and decide that it's probably easiest if I just roll out of it and crawl over to the movies which are pretty much at ground level anyway.

There's about a hundred movies here ranging from romance to terror. So I close my eyes, reach out and grab the first one I touch. "Is a comedy ok with everyone?"

Everyone nods so I take it out of its jacket and slip it into the side of his big screen TV. Jessy fluffed up my beanbag chair while I was picking the movie. I settle back into it again. He hands me my bag of chips and the black licorice whips that I couldn't pass up when we were picking our treats.

Reilly reaches up and flips off the light, and the movie begins.

CHAPTER

EIGHT

I love math. Math comes easily to me. Numbers revolve around everything we do in our lives. They're a definite when everything else can be altered. They're universal. For instance, language can be turned into slang and still have the same meaning. Numbers cannot, they are either the right number or the wrong one. They just make sense to me.

It's 2:30 PM and I have one class left. It's called Concentration Class. I'm a little nervous. Whenever I concentrate on anything too long, I tend to get a headache. I'm really hoping that's not what it's all about.

Todd's waiting outside of my math class. He smiles one of his pretty-boy smiles and slides his arm through mine. "Can I walk you to class? I figured since we both are on our way to the same class, we might as well walk together. Is that's ok with you, beautiful girl?"

Wow, two really hot guys touched me today. I never get this much attention. They're just being nice to the new kid. "Sure. I'm a little nervous so being with someone familiar will probably help."

It doesn't take us long to get to our class. Our casual conversation while we walk makes it seem really short. Todd can be a nice, normal guy when he wants to be.

I feel a calming warmth swoon over me as I enter the room. My fear and nervousness is gone. Now I remember why, Todd has the ability to control emotions and temperatures. I really am thankful that he's here. "You're helping me, aren't you?"

"Is that ok?" His voice is soothing and smooth. He must feel the flush of my nervous heat because he smiles his sexy little crooked smile.

"Definitely! Can you sit near me?" I don't think I've blinked since we entered the room until Todd's eyes meet mine and linger for just a fraction of a moment too long for it to feel like a casual glance.

He's still smiling at me. "We have to leave the backpacks, purses, books, basically everything against this wall. Make sure your cellphone is off or she'll throw you out of class if it rings." I do what he tells me. He points me in the direction of the back of the room.

The room looks more like a yoga workout gym with mats thrown about the carpeted classroom floor. The candles, blackboards and speakers that are scattered about the room convince me that it's probably not actually meant for yoga.

The walls are burgundy with candle sconces about every two meters apart with big white candles burning softly. The floor has five landings, each one raised about a foot up from the other. Each is wide enough to accommodate a full grown man quite easily. They step up towards the back of the room.

We walk up to the top tier and sit on two mats that are about midway across the room. Three other students sit along the top tier with us. Each one smiles and introduces themselves to me.

The first guy, Jerry, says he can hear things that most people can't hear. He's what's known as a Listener.

The second guy, Andy, says that he's a Progressionist. He can make a seed grow into a tree in a matter of hours. I think that's really cool.

The third person is a girl about fourteen years old. Her name is Rebecca. She's really shy. Her ability is to set things on fire but she hasn't learned how to put them out yet. She's still new here.

As others introduce themselves, I can't help but feel a little overwhelmed. There's so much information so fast. It is nice to know that there is a wide range of talents at this school. Some are weirder than mine. Maybe there are others like me and I just haven't been introduced yet. If everyone is still learning the extent of what their talents consist of, then who knows, there could be more.

"The instructors name is Maria Suvert. She prefers us to just call her Maria because she says it removes the uncomfortable tension assumed by having to address someone with a salutation. She's a very easy going person. Everyone likes her." Todd's sitting on a blue mat that he's pulled over to be right next to mine.

I don't mind the closeness. He's stunningly handsome, besides, he is keeping me calm. His gift is really coming in handy for me today.

Once everyone is seated and quiet, the instructor introduces herself to me and fills the class in on who I am and what my ability is. Yup, good thing Todd is keeping my fear level down to a minimal because I think I might otherwise have run screaming from the room.

Being the center of attention is not something I do well with. Thanks to Todd, I might avoid vomiting.

Note to self: Bring Todd with me to help out in nervous situations.

Maria then gives me a quick rundown of how in this class I will learn techniques of how to relax myself so that when I have an episode, I'll be able to keep myself calm through it. That might help me see more details in the vision and could help with the pain level.

I really hope this works. Not so much for the details of the vision, more for the pain level. If I can ease that, I'll be a happy girl. Maybe this will help with the anxiety that I feel when I know that these attacks are coming. I call them attacks because I think it's a more suitable word than episode or vision. At least right now that's what they seem like.

We lie out on the mats and begin a deep breathing exercise to help us get into a more relaxed state. Todd must still be helping my mood because if I relax anymore, I'll be asleep.

Todd reaches out and touches my hand. OhmyGod this sexy, amazing guy wants to hold my hand. He interlaces our fingers and instantly more warmth soothes through my body so intensely. I can feel it radiating from his hand and flowing into mine, down my arm, then spread throughout my body. It's like having an invisible warm blanket covering all of me.

The warmth is increasing and the relaxing feeling is changing to... desire? The heat is changing into desire? More and more my sexual excitement is building. I can almost feel his breath on me, so hot, heating me up. I want him to touch me, touch me in places never yet touched by a boy. I want him kissing me, caressing me, on me.

My mouth is open, I'm breathing heavier and faster. Why can't I tell him to stop? If he touches my body right now, I'll melt into a heaping pile of heated flesh and yet still yearn for more. I'll be unable to stop myself from going too far, farther than I consciously want to go. A soft moan flows from deep within me and escapes my lips.

Just then, that feeling is gone. At first I feel angry, I want it back. Then I'm left wondering what the heck happened and where did that come from? Suddenly I'm overcome with a feeling of satisfaction, not my emotion, someone else's. It's the kind of satisfaction of a job well done. Todd's gloating. He's proud of his accomplishment, I can feel it.

I open my eyes and turn my head only to meet Todd's sexy eyes. I pull my hand away when I finally realize that he was making me feel that way. It's obvious that he's thinking that I'd like it and want him to do it again, maybe later when we're not in class. I'm kind of angry that he forced himself into invading me in such a way but at the same time, I kind of do want him to do it again. I've never felt so sexy, so filled with desire, so wanted.

Looking at his smug face really ruins it though. I can't believe how weak I must be to let him control me like that, so easily. Maybe other girls like it when he controls them like that but I don't.

"Don't do that again." I whisper to him trying to sound angry but through my still heavy breathing, it sounds like I didn't really mean it.

Still his bedroom eyes are looking deep into mine. Through his sexy grin he replies, "Did you not like that because it sure looked as if you were absolutely enjoying it. Perhaps this just isn't the place for it. Maybe in a more sccluded place next time."

"No next time. There won't be a next time. If I ever feel that way again around you, it'd better be because I want to feel like that, not because you're forcing it on me. Understand?" I glare at him. Even though I secretly do want him to do it again. I try to mask that feeling with anger. I really hope he can't sense that I truly did enjoy it.

He raises an eyebrow at me then turns his head so he's looking at the ceiling, folds his arms over his chest and closes his eyes, still with a smirking little smile. "So what you're saying is that you want me to do it again, but only on your terms? I can deal with that."

No matter how hard I try to relax and get back into the exercise, I'm not able to. I just can't decide if I'm angry at him or if he's right and I really do want him. Thankfully there's only ten minutes left of the class.

I start walking down the hallway as quick as I can, desperate not to make a scene but still trying to get away from Todd. But before I can get far, he's walking beside me, keeping up with my pace, quite easily I might add. Of course he is taller than me with longer legs. Why did I think I could get away?

"Do you forgive me?" He doesn't really sound like he cares if I actually forgive him or not. And when I don't say anything, just nod my head, he smiles at me with the most adorable little boy 'forgive-me' smile. He looks so innocent but now I know better.

Instead of going straight to my room, I stop at Tara's door and knock. "Come on in." Tara's sitting on her bed reading a book. "Hi Laura, how'd your first Concentration Class go?"

"Well, that's why I'm here. The class was great. I think I'm going to learn a lot. The teacher, Maria, she seems awesome. I want to ask you something about Todd though."

Tara drops her head down and with a muffled sound she asks me, "What did he do now?"

"He controlled my moods." I reply, rolling my eyes.

She lifts her head to look at me. "How did he make you feel?"

"I was seconds away from doing the nasty with him right there in the middle of the classroom with everyone there. I moaned out loud. Thankfully he stopped! Then I felt his self-satisfaction." I pause and Tara rolls her eyes. "I must admit, it was hot. I've never felt that way before, even with my boyfriend, Brian."

Tara is trying not to laugh but she's unsuccessful. Through her snickering, she says,

"He can be so bad." She stops giggling and seriously asks me, "So you've never... you know, done it?"

"Nope. I really don't want to yet. I don't think I'm ready for something that heavy yet. I mean, I've never felt the desire to with Brian. I don't think he's mature enough to handle it. I think that when I'm ready, I won't have any doubts, so I'll know." I pause for a second then ask her, "Have you ever..?"

"Once, about a year ago with a boy named Steven. Not here at Salvation. I wasn't here yet. Steven and I were an item when it happened. We dated for about three years before we did it. We got into making out in his room one day while his parents were at work. We had a day off school. It was all planned out and everything. We made love, sort of. It was clumsy and awkward. I always pictured it playing out as a romantic adventure where the two of us would bond even more than ever. I just knew in my heart that it would be everything I'd ever hoped for. Well, it was nothing like I thought it would be."

"That's what I'm afraid of. I'd like my first time to be an event to remember, something to look back on fondly. Not like what happened with you." I'm hoping that I'm not offending her. "Besides, Brian and I definitely aren't there yet."

"Back to what Todd did to you..." She's giggling a bit again. "At least he did something awesome with you. He was really bad with me. He built up so much impatience and anxiety in me that I got up and stormed out of class. That was how I actually met Todd. I had no idea that he could do that or even who he was."

"Wow, what an ass. So what happened next?" I am now very glad that 'impatience and anxiety' was not the emotion that he filled me with. At least mine was pleasurable, very pleasurable.

"He chased me out of the classroom and filled me with calmness then he explained what he did and apologized. Needless to say, I didn't like Todd all that much at first. He really is a nice guy once you get to know him. Todd would give you the shirt off his back if you needed it. Just don't trust whatever you 'feel' when you're around him." Tara shrugs her shoulders.

We chat for a bit then set a time to head down for dinner. I leave her room and travel a whole ten steps to my room. I'm so glad to be back in my new sanctuary, safe from all the strangeness this place exudes.

It feels like there's something leery hanging in the air. Something's not quite right. It's almost as though I'm waiting for the ceiling to fall down on me or something. Maybe it's just my own anxieties of being in a new place with new people.

I splash some cold water on my face and brush my teeth because they're feelin' like fuzzy slippers. I sit down on my bed and start taking my books out of my backpack when someone taps on my door. It must be Tara... she's early.

CHAPTER

NINE

"Come on in, doors open." But then I remember that the doors are always open here. We have locks but nobody ever locks the doors because if something happens, people need to have access to you and a locked door makes that really hard to do. This is a hospital after all.

It isn't Tara, its Laden, the smokin' hot orderly. "Hi. I just want to stop by and check in on you. Can I come in?"

OhmyGod, mega hot Laden is actually standing in my room. Since the door has a hinge making it close automatically, he's here in my room, alone, with me, with the door closed. "Yeah, come in. Have a seat." I don't point to the chair or beside me on the bed. I'm not sure where I want him to sit. My heart is pounding. My body's heating up and I'm getting flush, I can feel it.

If he sits on the bed, I know that after what happened today, I'll probably try to kiss him. How embarrassing will it be if I make a move on him and he rejects me because he thinks of me as just a kid? He is older than me after all. Not a lot older, but still.

Laden takes the chair from my desk and turns it so that he's facing me. The chair is so close to me that when he is sits our knees are touching.

He asks, "Can I take your blood pressure and check your heart rate? I don't know if the nurses have explained to you why we're checking so often. They usually don't unless you ask." When I shake my head no, Laden continues, "Well, two reasons really. First, we want to make sure you're healthy and stay that way. Second, if we can get any different fluctuations in your vitals charted, maybe we'll know when a vision will happen and you can prepare yourself for it. That'd be great, huh?"

Laden looks deeply into my eyes. His baby blues make my stomach flutter. He smiles his sexy smile. Funny thing is, I don't think he's trying to smile sexy, his face just is sexy.

I nod, awkwardly. I wanted to say something like, 'you can check my vitals anytime you'd like' or 'please stay here and never leave' but it only came out sounding like an idiotic grunting exhale. I immediately feel the hot flush of redness overcome my face.

He smiles again but quickly drops his eyes and tries to erase his grin, trying not to embarrass me. Laden shuffles with the paperwork and says, "The nurses are really busy today and since I'm doing my nursing rotation, they asked if I'd help them out by checking your vitals... all the kids on this floor, not just you. If you'd rather have a certified nurse do it, I won't be offended."

Of course I want him to take my vitals! I want him to touch me just like he did the last time I saw him. I think my arm is still tingling. "I don't mind. I'm sure you know what you're doing." Who cares if he knows what he's doing or not. I stick my arm out so that he can wrap the blood pressure thing around my arm and suddenly realize why he's fighting off a laugh. So I add quickly, "When you're taking vitals... I'm sure you know what you're doing for taking vitals." I should have just shut up when I had the chance because a giggle does escape his lips.

He keeps glancing up after he wraps the pressure cuff around my arm and begins pumping it up. Our eyes keep meeting every time I try to catch a glimpse of his stunning face, perfect lips or silky golden hair.

Laden takes the stethoscope out of his ears then he takes off the arm wrap and writes on the clipboard. He stands up and puts the stethoscope ear pieces near his ears. "Can I listen to your heart?" He gestures for me to let him stick the cold stethoscope under my shirt.

Of course I nod, he is studying to become a nurse and I should definitely be his practice dummy. My stomach is flipping crazily and my mind is racing with all kinds of thoughts.

My face must be blood red. I can just imagine what the readings for my heart rate and blood pressure are. I can feel my heart ready to pound out of my chest. If he stands close enough to me, he won't even need that stethoscope. I take a few deep breaths trying to slow it down before he listens.

He sticks the stethoscope at the top left side of my back then to the other side. He brings his arm around to the front of my t-shirt.

Hesitating slightly, he carefully slides his hand and the stethoscope under the collar of my shirt to the upper right side of my chest. I inhale hard but can't seem to exhale. His touch is so gentle yet firm. A quiver rushes over me. I close my eyes in an attempt to calm myself down.

Maybe if I'm not looking at his perfect body standing right in front of me as he leans over me and I picture some old ugly doctor guy, then maybe my heart rate will go back to normal. But no, that's obviously not going to happen. I exhale hard, making a weird noise.

"Take a deep breath for me." He asks… I comply. He moves over to the upper left side of my chest. "Again…" I inhale again. He moves the stethoscope under my shirt down my left side just below my breast. "Can you take one more breath for me?" All I can think is 'OhmyGod, maybe'!

Somehow I manage to inhale once more so he pulls his hand out of my shirt then sits back down. He goes to write something down on the clipboard and stops. He looks up at me nervously. "Um, your heart rate is really high. Is that because of me?" He's looking straight into my eyes so serious but in a charming, vulnerable way.

Ok… so, I thought my heart was going to pound out of chest before, well I think it definitely will right now. I can hear it in my ears, loud. "Maybe." I'm not going to say no, that will be a lie and I fear he'll know it. I'm suddenly very aware that my eyes are wide open, much larger than normal so I try to adjust but only end up blinking a few times.

He lays the clipboard down on the desk, puts his hand on my cheek and stares into my eyes. He pulls my face towards his. His lips stop about a millimeter from my lips. OhdearGod please don't let me puke.

Then our lips touch, soft at first, then he full on kisses me.

His lips feel exactly as I'd imagined so many times before. I thought they'd feel soft, warm, gentle... I was right. My lips part with his and we mesh them together. His tongue softly explores my mouth. My tongue tenderly stroking his...

His chest touches mine as he lays me back onto my bed with him on top of me. Our lips are frantically kissing. My fingers weave their way through his hair. My other arm is tightly wrapped around his shoulder, as though I'm holding him to me, fearful that if I let go, he'll disappear and this will have only been a dream.

Is this really happening or am I imagining this? Holy Crap, I think it's real.

He supports his weight with his one arm so he doesn't crush me and his other hand is under me, holding my butt. His body somehow slid in between my legs. His hips are gently rocking. The firmness I feel is a full reminder that he is a man. His hand leaves my ass and slides up under my shirt and under my bra. He shifts his weight then his other hand lifts my shirt. His lips leave mine and kiss down to the base of my neck. Reality slaps me... I don't know if I'm ready for this.

A knock on the door shatters the moment and we spring off the bed, both of us frantically trying to compose ourselves. We are both breathing heavily and trying to gain control of ourselves. I manage to yell out, "I'll be right there."

Did that just happen? I almost went to second base in only about five minutes. Ok, so I'm turning into one of 'those' girls. I thought I had more control over myself.

Note to self: Control yourself!

I take a quick look in the mirror as I run my fingers through my hair in a failed attempt to smooth it. I open the door only a bit.

Todd is standing there. I thought it would be Tara but I can never be that lucky. Please dear God don't let him feel my emotions. Oh please, oh please. He'll know something's up.

"Oh, I must have fallen asleep. I'll be out in a minute. Are you headed down to the mess hall?" I don't know what to say. Why is he here anyways?

"Are you ok? You look flushed. Your anxiety is really high too. Are you having a migraine?" He's looking at me rather intensely, curiously.

I shake my head, maybe too vigorously. "I'm fine. No migraine. I was just sleeping and you startled me awake. Why are you here anyways? You shouldn't be here." That comes out a little too abruptly. Not my intention.

"Um, I thought maybe I could come in and we could talk about what happened in Concentration Class." Todd's waiting a moment for me to respond, but I don't know what to say to him. "Can I come in? Are you sure you're ok?"

"No! I mean yes, wait, I'm really alright." That was a really quick response, too quick. Now he's looking at me weird. What do I say so that he doesn't want to come in. "My rooms a mess and besides, I don't trust you enough to be alone with you. Not after today. I'm sure you understand why."

"Yeah, no problem, I understand. Are we good?" He really does look apologetic. I nod ok. "Good. Ok. I'll see you downstairs for dinner. It's pizza and lasagna night."

After I nod again, Todd slowly walks away. And I shut the door. That was so close. I inhale and exhale deeply.

I turn around to see how Laden is doing but jump when he plants a kiss on me. He was standing right behind me the whole time that I was talking to Todd. No wonder Todd was looking at me so weird, he was probably reading Laden too and had no idea.

Laden's body pushes me against the door. His hands slide under my butt and lift me up, opening my legs around him. I wrap them tightly around his hips, lacing my feet at his back.

Laden grinds his pelvis into me. His muscles are flexed and strong, holding me. His lips, warm and velvety, kiss my neck. This is so hot, it's so bad. Naughty! This is so not me!

I think I'm even more excited just knowing that a simple door is between us and the rest of the world. He can't be seen with me, not like this, he would lose his job and maybe even his career. Not to mention that people would think I'm a slut, after all, I just got here.

Another knock at the door and I jump and squeal a little. "Laura, it's me, Tara. Are you just about ready?"

"I need a few minutes. If you want to go on down without me, that's ok, I'll catch up soon."

"No, I can wait. Are you getting dressed or can I come in?" Tara is so impatient.

"I'm getting dressed. Just a second, ok?" I'm desperate to keep her out in the hall.

Laden puts me down and moves away from the door and whispers, "She's obviously not going to leave without you so why don't you go and I'll hang out here until I'm sure the coast is clear, then I'll slip out."

Sounds like a good plan to me. I run my fingers for the second time, through my hair. I check my make-up and decide to just wipe most of it off, no time to put more on. It doesn't help when my eyes are red anyway. But when I go to grab the door handle, Laden grabs my hand and pulls me close to him.

"I'll catch up with you another time. Maybe we can continue where we left off or we can just hang out." Laden is sooo hot! I can't believe this is happening. He releases my hand so I open the door just enough for me to slide out and let it close behind me.

Dinner was great. Maybe that's because I'm still super giddy from what happened with Laden. Not only was the food awesome but I'm getting to know my group of new friends better. I like them, they're fun.

I'm finally in my room, alone. I have some time to myself. I decide to get caught up on my emails. I flip open my computer and wake it from its sleep. I open my Facebook account, read up on what my friends are doing and throw out a few comments on their posts.

Ronny is the only one who's messaged me through Facebook. Not Brian though. He hasn't changed his status in three days. I think he's avoiding me.

I fire off a quick note to Ronny giving him a quick rundown of how it's going here so far, leaving out the part about Laden, of course. He's just worried that I'm lonely, scared or that they're doing weird experiments on me. I let him know that the experiments are performed at a minimum. Then tell him that I'm only kidding, no experiments. I make it a point to tell him that I still have no answers as to why this is happening to me. Hopefully soon I will.

I open my email account. There are two messages from my mom and one from Brian. I read and reply back to my mom's email first.

I'm not going to fill her in on exactly what's going on here. How would I explain it anyways? Oh, by the way mom, I made out with a hot nurse guy who's older than me... I don't think so!

I open Brian's email and read it. He's breaking up with me. Ok, I know that I shouldn't feel angry or hurt, especially because of the way that I carried on with Laden, but I am. I'm hurt. I email him back saying that I agree with him anyway and close up my email. I can't believe he wasn't even man enough to do it in person... or even over the phone.

I shut down my computer, then climb into bed, try to put Brian out of my mind and with the relaxation techniques that I learned, I'm able to force myself to sleep.

CHAPTER

TEN

Beep, beep, beep. Ugh, my Blackberry is beeping away, someone's texting me. I roll over to look at the clock and can't believe that someone is waking me up at 6:45 am. It takes me a few minutes to get my bearings.

Beep, beep, beep. "Fine! I hear you already!" I snatch up my phone to see who's bugging me. It's Tara.

I click the message to find out what she thinks is so incredibly important that she can't wait another fifteen minutes until the tap on the door would wake me up. Ok, so yeah, I'm a little grouchy this morning. I could have had another fifteen minutes of sleep.

Her message reads, 'I'll pick you up at 7:10 so I can show you around the school before breakfast.'

The next message read, 'r u up yet?'

The third message read, 'u can't ignore me all day.'

Beep, beep, beep another message just coming in, 'ok, I'm coming over to get you up!'

I quickly text back 'No!' and hit return. Quickly writing 'I'm up! 7:20 is ok' and hit return. Growling under my breath, I force myself out of bed and hit the bathroom for a quick shower.

Sure enough at 7:15 Tara taps at my door. "Come on in. I just have to brush my teeth, you're early."

The door pops open and Tara comes bouncing in with two coffees in her hands and a paper. "Nope, I said 7:10 and you said 7:20 so I compromised. I figured you can use a coffee. You seem a little grumpy this morning. Here's some mail for you. It was in your slot."

I take the paper from her and read it over while I brush. 'Please come to room #19 at 9 this morning. I'm looking forward to meeting you. Dr. Jennifer Adams'.

"Who is Dr. Jennifer Adams? What's her story?" How Tara can understand me with toothpaste in my mouth baffles me.

"She's really nice. I like her. She relaxes you enough so that you can use your gift to the best of your potential. Like for me, she helps me to leave my body and guides me in my travels. She's the one who helped me realize that I can hear what people are saying when I'm travelling. I didn't know that before. I only knew that I could see what people were doing. She helped me figure it out. Are you just about ready to go? We're running out of time here." Tara explains as I hear her shuffling around the bedroom.

I rinse my mouth, throw my purse over my shoulder and stare at her as she's finishing making my bed. I can't believe she made my bed… she's so nice. "You went down to the mess hall and got us coffee and you make my bed for me? Alright, I forgive you for waking me up early. Thank you."

Tara giggles, "No problem. Dr. Jennifer, as she likes to be called, might be able to help you see the more important things in your visions, not just the awful things, like death and bodies... eww. Maybe she'll help you learn how to slow the visions down, like in slow motion or something. You did say it was like watching a movie. Maybe it works the same way… play, rewind, fast forward, pause…"

I hope Tara's right. I don't want to be so focused on the horrible stuff. Maybe if I can see through all that, then I might be able to prevent them from happening in the first place.

We wander around the hospital while she tells me about each room and usually some kind of story that goes along with it, until we come to a room with 'Restricted' written in red letters across the door. Tara stops and stares at the door.

"We aren't allowed in there, we being non-hospital staff. As you can see, we'd need a keycard. I sure would like to get in there though." Tara seems to lose herself in thought. "It's weird how we're allowed pretty much anywhere in this place but we're not allowed to go through this door. I just wonder what is so important in there that it has to be locked away. What are they hiding? I mean, locking the door only makes us more curious."

"So what's the big deal, so they lock it, so what? It's probably just patient records, storage or maybe that's just where they lock up the staff's purses and junk. Most places provide a spot for employees to lock up their personal items while they work."

Tara walks closer to me and whispers, "If that's the case, and don't look now, but why would they need a locked door and a camera?" She rolls her eyes up over her head directing me where the camera is. "Theft has never been a problem here. I mean, we don't even lock our doors and our computers and other expensive things are in our rooms. As for the camera, why aren't there more of them installed all around the whole hospital and school area? Why just here, in front of this door?" Tara crosses her arms and taps her toe on the floor making a light tapping noise.

"Yeah, ok, that is weird. Has anyone ever asked?"

"Sure, but the staff just tell us to leave it alone and stop asking questions. That just makes me want to ask more questions. I'm just nosey like that." Tugging on the arm that's not holding my almost empty cup of coffee, she adds, "Let's get out of here before someone comes and escorts us out."

"Hey Tara why don't you just drift through the Restricted door?" I ask.

"Oh, no. I never go where I'm not invited. That would be rude. At least that's how I was raised. I don't know. I never actually thought about it. I guess it's worth thinking about, maybe." Tara seems scared kind of like a kid about to get caught with their hand in the candy drawer.

As we wander back through the corridors on our way to the mess hall, Tara continues with the tour. I'll never remember everything she tells me, but it gives me a good start. It doesn't look like I'll get lost to easily if I ever have to go to this area again. The floor plan is pretty easy to catch onto.

Breakfast is great. I have my Lucky Charms Cereal and some fruit while everyone tells me about their stories of how the wonderful Dr. Jennifer helps them out. I really am looking forward to meeting with her in…

"OhmyGod! I have five minutes to get to Dr. Jennifer's office. I have to go guys." Everyone looks up at the clock and shoots up out of their chairs too. Everyone lost track of time and we are all going to be late.

Note to self: Appoint someone to be the time-watcher.

I almost run down the corridor to room #19. I suck in a deep breath in an attempt at trying to slow my heart rate down before I rap on the door. Under her name is a sign hanging from a chain that says 'open for visitors'. Tap, tap.

"Come on in Darlin'." I open the door and step inside. Before I can close the door, she asks, "Sweetie can you just flip that sign over please and thank you."

I flip the sign and read that side, 'silence please, come back later'. I shut the door quietly behind me.

Her room looks like an old library with hundreds of books that line the wall, floor to ceiling, on dark wood shelving. Her desk looks as though it were hand carved, matching the big wooden chair that sits behind it. The floor has an old-style wool rug that stretches almost the full length of the room. The lazy boy chair looks like the only thing in here that's made in this era.

Walking toward me is a short woman in her mid-fifties but with a full head of grey hair. She can't possibly weigh more than ninety pounds soaking wet. Her smile is big and friendly, just like my friends had said it was. I can't help but smile back at her.

She takes the purse from over my shoulder and sets it down on the table beside the door. "So you're Laura, huh? Well, it's nice to finally put a face to the name. I'm Dr. Jennifer Adams but please just call me Dr. Jennifer, ok?"

"Hi, it's nice to meet you too. Have you read all these books?" Most of the books look really old and well worn.

"Yup, every single one of them. Took me a lot of years too. Please, take a load off." She points at the lazy boy as she walks back to her desk.

I sit in the big burgundy lazy boy as she goes on explaining why I'm here. "Well Laura, I'm here to try and help you learn how to use your gift in such a way that you'll get the most out of it. I figure that there must be some cosmic reason why all you kids are having these afflictions. Maybe you all are here to save the world one day. Maybe it's all the preservatives that are being put in our food now-a-days. Who knows? But if it is to save the world then I would like you all to have the best knowledge you can possibly have so the world doesn't cave in and kill us all." She giggles.

Dr. Jennifer has a way of putting things. I like her. She's a normal type of person, straight forward, no bullshit. Maybe while she's learning all she can learn from me, I can learn as much as I can from her. After all, if she's read this many books on psychological studies, I should really pay attention.

My mind shifts back to the 'Restricted' room that Tara showed me earlier and no matter how hard I try, I just can't imagine Dr. Jennifer being up to some mid-evil plot against us kids. I truly don't think she has an evil bone in her body.

"Ok, let's get started, shall we? Flip the leg-rest up and lay back my dear. Take a break. I'm sure you could use one." Again with the giant smile. "We'll start every session with deep breathing, kind of like when you're in Concentration Class but if you fall asleep here, I shoot spitballs at you until you wake up." Giggles come from both of us. She can't be serious… although, she might be.

"Start with some deep breathing and I'll talk, you focus in on my voice, ok? Then I'll ask you some questions and you can answer them the best way you can without thinking too hard." I start breathing deeply while she's talking.

"I'd like you to imagine that you're standing directly in front of a huge wall and on this wall is nothing but white paint. Imagine yourself reaching your hand out and touching the white wall. Now I'd like you to imagine turning your head to the left. You'll see that the white wall curves all the way around. Now I'd like you to imagine turning your head to the right and see the white wall curves all the way around to your right. Now imagine turning your head up towards the sky. Imagine that the white wall is really high. Imagine that the ceiling is also painted white. Now I'd like you to keep breathing deeply and take a step backwards.

The wall is still white. Take a few more steps backward. Imagine that you can see colours and shapes. Take a few more steps backwards. Now turn your head to the left and see now that the walls have something on them. Turn your head to the right. Something is on that wall too. When you look straight forward and take a few more steps back, the picture starts to come in clearer. Can you see a picture forming?"

I can actually see something. How is she doing this? "Yeah."

"Take a few more deep breaths, when you're comfortable enough, take a few more steps back. Look all around you and when you feel like you can, start describing what you see on the walls."

I take a few steps back and realize where I am, I'm in the food court; the same food court that I saw collapse in my last vision. "I'm scared. I have to get out of here!" Panic is starting to take over me.

"You are perfectly safe. Nothing can hurt you. Remember that you are only looking at painted walls. When you get scared, take a step forward and everything will stop. When you feel like you can continue, take a step back again."

I take a deep breath and look around the food court. "There's a woman in front of me with two little kids, twins maybe, about three years old. There's an old man eating alone. A group of girls are about thirteen years old. Three men in work clothes eating kind of fast."

"I'd like you to look around and read signs. Is there a sign with the name of a city on it? Is there a sign with the name of the mall? Do you see a store or restaurant with a name that you don't recognize? Remember that you can turn your head and look all around you. You can walk around and look for a sign. Maybe there is one around the next corner."

"I can't move. My body can't move. I don't see anything saying what city I'm in. There is a store called 'Campichamps', I don't recognize the name at all. There's no other sign." I feel like I'm watching a movie, from inside the movie film. This is amazing.

"Now, take another look around to see if anything looks out of the ordinary. Is there anything out of place or threatening in any way?" I can hear Dr. Jennifer, but her voice sounds hallow and like it's really far away, getting farther away. I have to concentrate more and more to hear her. I try to stay with her.

"There's a worker with a big plastic bin on wheels and he's putting trash in it while he pushes it through the food court. I guess that's not out of place." I start to take another look around when the floor starts to shake, then stops. "The floor shook! People are looking around at one another. The floor is shaking again! Everyone is getting up. Dust is falling from the ceiling. The floor is shaking really hard and the ceiling is starting to fall down. Oh no! Those kids, their Mom! They're under a big slab of ceiling. OhmyGod!"

"Laura, take a step forward then take a deep breath in." Dr. Jennifer's faint voice shocks me back to realizing that it is not really happening, that it's just like a movie, not real.

A haze fills the food court then little by little the scene unfolds through the dust and floating debris. It instantly slows down when I take a slow step forward, towards the movie screen, so to speak.

I continue talking to Dr. Jennifer, describing what I see. "I'm ok. It doesn't look like a bomb went off or anything like that. It looks like an earthquake has shaken the building so hard that the ceiling has fallen down. That's what it is. There must be a really big earthquake about to hit somewhere."

Confident that I will not be afraid, or at least trying to tell myself that, I take a step back.

Blackness engulfs me. Colours rush past me until I'm being thrown through the bubble. The scene immediately starts to play right where it left off from. I blink hard trying to force myself to not look at the bodies and the blood. I try to only look straight or up, not down.

"There are huge chunks of cement from the ceiling on top of people. The railing that surrounds the second floor has partially fallen. I don't know if anyone fell from there." I talk hoping that Dr. Jennifer can still hear me.

I turn my face to the left and scream loud enough that I shock myself. Horror! I see something that scares me so much that I scream louder than I ever have in my whole life.

In a matter of a split second, I'm being sucked out of the bubble, back through the colours into the blackness. My eyes fly open spinning me back to reality. Even though I'm awake and sitting up in the safety of the lazy boy chair, I'm still screaming, shaking and trying to run away. If my legs weren't so shaky, I just might have been able to. I've never been so terrified in all my life.

Dr. Jennifer has my face in her hands and she's looking straight into my eyes. "You're ok, nothing can hurt you here. When you think you can… tell me, what did you see?"

I'm still panting and crying. I try to tell her. "A man… he was bleeding really badly. His ear was hanging off and he had blood coming out of his mouth. He was covered in blood… all over his clothes. It's the same man that I saw eating alone."

I can't help but sob. The horror of seeing that man is being changed into sadness. He must hurt so badly. It looks so painful. "He scared the hell out of me. Why was he standing there? Why next to me?"

Dr. Jennifer hands me some Kleenex and tries to comfort me. "The man can't hurt you. He doesn't even know that you're there. Remember that you were only witnessing the event and not actually participating in it."

I look up at her and my eyes feel heavy. "Then why did he look right at me and say, 'Young lady, can you help me?'"

All the blood seems to be leaving Dr. Jennifer's face. Her eyes are huge and her mouth is moving but words aren't coming out. She stands and walks quickly over to the window and whips open the drapes, blasting sunshine throughout the room. My eyes are burning. I can hardly hold them open.

I wait quietly for what seems like ten minutes but is probably more like two until she stops scanning the books on her shelves before she actually says anything.

"Did he actually talk to you or do you think that just by coincidence he might be talking to someone that you can't see? Perhaps someone is standing on the other side of you?" Dr. Jennifer is leaning on her desk looking back at her books. I think she's searching for a particular one.

"He was talking to me. There was nobody else around me, I'm sure of it. He was standing right beside me. I could have touched him if I was actually there. It scared the shit out of me. I don't want that to happen again. It won't happen again, right?" I am desperate for her to tell me, to promise me, that indeed it never will. But she doesn't. She stares at me for moment but doesn't say anything. I take that to mean that it probably will happen again.

"I have read about this before, I've personally never experienced having a patient do it. If I could just find that particular book... Here it is." She takes the book from one of the lower shelves and holds it gently. She's smiling at it like it's an old friend that she hasn't seen in a very long time.

The cover is brown with small printed words on the front that I can't read from so far away. When she opens the book it makes a crackling sound. It is obviously extremely old. The pages are yellowish and the writing is very faded.

"Can I use the bathroom? I'd really like to splash some cold water on my face." Before she even says that I can, I'm up out of the lazy boy and picking up my purse, heading to the little washroom that's just past her desk. She doesn't say whether I can use it or not, she's too busy carefully flipping pages. Her lips move silently as she reads little bits off each of the page, searching for something in particular.

I look into the mirror and can't believe how horrible I look. My eyes are so bloodshot and the reddish-purple under my eyes is even more emphasized by the intense paleness of my skin. I splash some water on my face and decide to use the toilet while I'm in there.

I hear Dr. Jennifer mumbling from the other room. I hope she doesn't think that I'm still sitting in the chair and that she's talking to me. She is pretty engrossed in that book, so maybe she does.

I shudder when I picture that man's bloody face so close to mine. I just can't believe that I didn't pee my pants. The way his ear was hanging and the blood that was flowing down from his head was gruesome. My body shivers again.

I come out of the bathroom after several minutes. Dr. Jennifer is still flipping through the book. I ask her, "Is it ok if I go now? I don't want to do that again today, I really don't."

She looks up from her book and says, "I'm going to read through this book again and leave little notes on papers where important information is so that you can read those pages, if you want to, otherwise, I'll just fill you in on what I find out. Maybe we can learn something that might help us make your journeys much more pleasurable and not so terrifying."

Dr. Jennifer looks up at me and realizes that I'm just standing there looking too terrified to even consider purposely going back into that vision let alone ever think it may ever be even remotely pleasurable.

She drops her voice down and calmly adds, "If we can discover how to enable communication between you and someone else, if indeed he was actually talking to you, perhaps you'll be able to talk to him. It sounds impossible because you're not actually there in your physical person. It'll take me a day or two though."

"Is that a book about what's happening to me? Please tell me that someone else has been in this situation before." I am desperate for any help I can get.

"Well, there are theories and claims, but I don't think there has actually been any solid proof of being recognized in visions. I will keep searching though. If I find anything, I'll drop this book in your mail slot as soon as I'm finished with it. If you don't want to read it, drop it back off to me and leave me a note. We can schedule an appointment for you to come in and we'll discuss it." I turn to leave her office and she calls out to me, "Just wait a moment dear, I called to have your orderly, Laden, come walk you back to your room. I just don't want you alone right now in case this session brings on a migraine and throws you right back into a vision. Not that I think it will, but just to be on the side of caution."

She called Laden? Great! I look like death and he's coming to see me. So far, this day is just crapping all over me.

"Hello, hello." Laden comes strolling in the door all smiles, until of course he sees how awful I look. "Wow, you look like you've been given a beating. I hope you got a few good swings in. How do you feel?" He laughs then takes my wrist and begins counting my heartbeats. Then holds up his finger and tells me to follow it with my eyes while he moves it from left to right and back left again. Although it hurts, I can still do it.

He looks straight into my eyes. The whole world around us disappears. Until of course, he pulls down my bottom eyelids and tells me to look up.

"Yup, she's blown a few vessels in and around her eyes, but otherwise she seems ok. Even still, I'll take her back to her room and keep an eye on her for a while." He flashes me a glance and a wink.

Without even looking up from her book, Dr. Jennifer says, "Good to know that all is good with you Laura. Try not to think about what happened here today. Put it as far out of your mind as possible so that you don't have a nightmare tonight when you're sleeping. I'll pick up with you later Sweetheart."

And with that, Laden and I leave her office.

CHAPTER

ELEVEN

I'm lying in my bed with my light blue cotton t-shirt and fuzzy blue pajama pants on because Laden insists that I be as comfortable as possible. He puts a cold damp washcloth over my tired red eyes. It feels really good.

"You just relax for a little while. I'm going to stay with you in case you need me. If you happen to fall asleep and wake up and I'm not here, I'll be back very shortly with some lunch for us. If you're ok after that, then you can go to class. Or just stay here with me and I can really help you relax."

Reassuring me that what happened between us really did happen, Laden kisses my lips so soft and gentle. With my eyes covered by the washcloth, the kiss seems to be so much more intense. Butterflies flap wildly in my belly. He pulls my blanket up over me tucking it under my neck then sits down on my computer chair.

I ask, "Laden, why do you think that I'm having these visions now, at this stage in my life, even though I've never had one before?"

He answers, "That's a good question. I don't have a definitive answer but in my opinion, I think it has something to do with your age. Most of the kids here didn't have any abilities until after maturity. However, some kids are as young as thirteen." Laden pauses for a few seconds. "I've asked myself that question a lot. I have no answers for you but I'm working on it. No more talking, you rest."

I'm quiet for about a minute before I can stand it no more. "What are you going to do between now and lunchtime? Please don't just sit there and stare at me." I really hope he finds something to do to keep himself busy. "You really don't even have to stay, I feel fine."

"Ok, I tell you what... I'll go get my laptop so that I can work on some of my own school work while you sleep, that way I won't be staring at you. I'll be back in a few minutes. You stay in bed." With that said, Laden leaves my room.

It's so quiet and I'm so exhausted. I welcome sleep. I must have drifted off quickly because I don't even hear Laden come back in the room. Did I fall asleep? I take the washcloth off my eyes and look around. I guess

I didn't fall asleep. Where is Laden when I need him? I feel weird... queasy almost.

I flip the blanket off of me and slide out of bed. I step out of my door to see if Laden is out there talking at the nurses' station. If so I can tell him that I'd like to go to the mess hall and get a ginger ale or something.

When I open the door, the scene unfolds. In a heartbeat my fear level is at its highest. I'm not half asleep, I'm wide awake, sort of, I think. I turn to run back to my bed but my room isn't behind me anymore. I am asleep, I think, right?! Obviously I'm not getting out of this dream so I think I'll just get it over with quickly.

I step through the door into the food court in the mall. The ceiling has already collapsed and some people are screaming. Some are obviously dead and others are just standing in one place, just looking around. I think they're in shock. I tell myself to just breathe and it'll be over with soon.

Reluctantly I turn around to my left. Sure enough, there he is, the man with the bloody face. His ear is still hanging off his head, of course. Blood is all over him. I can smell it and it's nauseating me. Wait, I can smell in my dream?

He speaks, "Young lady, can you help me?"

I'm trying desperately not to run screaming from this man. I remember what Dr. Jennifer had said about maybe he's talking to someone else, not me. I turn around to look on the opposite side of me to see if anyone is standing there. There is no one.

I turn back to him. "Can you see me?"

"Of course I can. Since you're not hurt, maybe you can help me." The bloody man isn't trying to be scary. He can actually see me. I can talk to him and he hears me. How can this be?

"What can I do? I'm not really here. This is just my vision. Besides, my body is frozen and I can't move... see." I attempt to make a step figuring that I'm not going to be able to, but I do, my body can move. How can this be happening? I feel the urge to do something, but what?

I look down to see that I'm wearing the same light blue cotton t-shirt and fuzzy blue pajama pants that I was wearing when Laden tucked me into bed.

The bloody man takes my hand in his. OhmyGod! He can touch me. Am I actually here somehow? While pulling me along behind him, he starts to talk again. His voice is so soft and monotone. I think he's in shock. "I need you to come over here and help this woman."

"Wait! The best way that I can help you sir, is if you tell me where we are and what mall we are in. And tell me the date and the time. Please! I am seeing this from the past and I might be able to stop this from even happening. Do you understand?"

I can do something. I can help. That's why I'm here. That's why I can see these visions. They're not coming to me to scare me, it's because I'm supposed to prevent tragedies that are shown to me. I'm not scared of having visions anymore.

The bloody man tells me the time and date, and the city and the name of the mall. I thank him and wish him luck. I turn around to go back to the doorway that leads to my room, but where is that? There's no tunnel or hole that I'm supposed to climb through. Am I stuck here forever? Wait, I remember how I got out of the vision from earlier, when I first saw the bloody man. I screamed. That brought me out of the vision.

It can't hurt to try. I take a deep breath… I look up at the ceiling as straight and tall as I can, preparing for the pull back to my body. I close my eyes and scream as loud as I can.

Suddenly I'm weightless and being sucked backwards through the colours and then the blackness so fast that I want to throw-up. I open my eyes to see Laden sitting on my bed with his hands on my shoulders, shaking me and anxiously repeating my name.

"Laura! Laura, wake up! It's just a dream, come back to me." Laden looks scared. His eyes are huge and even in this very dim room I can see that he's a little pale.

"Ok, ok, stop shaking me, I'm back now. What happened?" I know what happened from my perspective but I want to know why he was shaking me. Did I scream bloody murder in this world too?

"You were sleeping and obviously dreaming but you didn't look like you were having a bad dream so I let you sleep. Then all of a sudden you sat up, looked up to the ceiling and screamed so loud. You scared the hell out of me! You just kept screaming until I shook you and you woke up. What the hell did you dream?" Laden still looks scared but the colour is starting to come back to his face.

"Is that a pop for me?" On my computer table is a tray full of food and what looks to be a nice cold pop. He opens it and hands it to me. I take a long drink and of course, burp. Yeah that's sexy. I apologize.

"I know where the vision takes place and when. I can prevent this. I have to tell someone."

Laden picks up his cellphone and punches in some numbers and hands me the phone. "Arianna Phillips, how can I help you?"

"Hi, it's Laura Sadie here. I had a vision earlier with Dr. Jennifer's guidance and just now, when I was asleep, I dreamed it again. But this time was different." For some reason my stomach goes all queasy when I try to tell her about the man talking to me and touching me and that I could walk around. I decide not to mention it. "I know when and where it's going to happen."

"Ok, first of all, how are you feeling?" Arianna is trying to keep her voice calm but I can hear the anxiousness that she's trying to repress.

"I'm fine, Laden is here with me and he checked my vitals." I wonder if I should have told her that but then realized that Dr. Jennifer was the one who told him to stay with me, so it's ok. "But I need to tell you where so you can make it not happen." I go on to tell her when and where I see my vision taking place.

"Laura, how did you get this information?" Arianna is really curious.

What do I tell her? I can't tell her the truth because my stomach flips around and won't let me every time I try to tell her. I have to lie but I'm so bad at it. "I'm not sure how I know. I just do. Maybe I saw a sign or something but I'm absolutely, positively sure that the information is true. I just deep down really believe it." I hope I sound convincing.

"Ok, don't you worry about a thing. I'll call the necessary people and we'll do everything we can to prevent this from happening. So you just rest and take care of yourself. If you have any symptoms arise then make sure you let Laden or Nurse Lorraine know about it." Arianna sounds so strong, so in control. I wish I were more like her.

I hang up the phone and hand it back to Laden "I'd really like to eat something. Is that our lunch?"

Laden grabs me and holds me to him. He wraps his arms around me and I melt into him. I really do need someone to hold me. Normally it'd be my mom but she's not here. I miss her.

After a few minutes, Laden releases me, kisses my forehead then reaches over and turns on the light. He puts the tray in front of me, pulls up a chair next to the bed, and leans in to kiss me but he stops abruptly. His eyes open huge and he pulls a penlight out of his pocket.

He shines the really obnoxiously bright light in and out of my line of vision.

"Can you look up? Down, to the left, now right?" Laden takes the light from my eyes. "Can you see alright? I mean, is your vision clear?"

Ok, now I'm getting scared. "No, I have a bunch of little red spots in them because of your penlight. Otherwise, yeah, why?" I hop up almost knocking the tray off the bed, quickly walk to the bathroom and flip on the light. I'm horrified by the reflection staring back at me.

My eyes look like balls of blood and the bags under my eyes are purple. I look like I've been punched in both eyes, a few times. All I can think about is what is everyone going to say when they see me? They're going to freak out. I look like a monster.

Laden comes into the bathroom and stands behind me with his hands on my shoulders. In comparison to my ugly mug, his face is as perfect as an angel's would be, maybe better. I still can't believe he likes me.

"Don't worry, Laura, it will go away in time. Come eat some lunch". Laden pulls me away from the mirror and guides me back to my bed to eat lunch.

Nurse Lorraine comes to my room. Wow, news really travels fast. Arianna must have called her and asked her to check on me. It's a good thing that Laden wasn't hugging me or kissing me when she walked in.

She does a quick blood pressure test and gives me a pill to take. She says that it will help me get some real sleep with no interruptions. I gladly take it. Sleep without dreams sounds amazing. I'm kind of scared to close my eyes. Maybe this pill will ease my anxiety and let me rest.

After I am almost forced to eat lunch, Laden insists that I lay back and rest. So I climb back under my covers and drift off into a dreamless sleep.

CHAPTER

TWELVE

I wake from my fantastic sleep. The sun is shining through the gaps in my curtains. The tap at the door is what woke me in the first place. I roll over and look at the clock, 6:57am.

I can't believe that I slept for more than 17 hours. The best part of my sleep is that there were no scary dreams, no airplanes crashing, no ceilings collapsing and no bloody faced men.

Beep, beep. My phone is alerting me. Tara must have texted me. I pick up my phone and sure enough, Tara sent me a text to make sure I'm awake and let me know that she'll be here in 45 minutes to pick me up for breakfast. I suppose I'd better get up then.

My body is so stiff from sleeping so long. I rub my eyes only to feel pain. I instantly remember that I look like a monster. I almost run to the bathroom and I flip on the light.

OhmyGod! I look the same as yesterday, a little better maybe. It wasn't just a horrible dream. The whites of my eyes are blood red, creepy, and the bags under my eyes are still an awful reddish colour. "Dammit!"

I quickly flip on my computer and fire off an apologetic email to my mom and dad letting them know that I had an episode so I was medicated and therefore slept forever and that's why I didn't email them last night. I didn't tell them about my eyes or what happened during my vision. They would only worry.

Tara and I get to the mess hall and everyone who glances our way, stops dead and stares at my eyes. I am the center of attention. If I wasn't so hungry, I'd just run back to my room and hide out until this goes away. Even Tara stared at me for a good five minutes before she looked away. I explained to her what I saw and was able to do during my vision. She was amazed.

Tara and I sit down at the breakfast table. Nobody looks up right away. Until, of course, when Jessy freaks out. "Holy Shit! What the hell happened to you?! If someone hurt you, I'm going to kick their ass. Tell me who it was." He spoke so loudly that people two tables over stop their conversations to look at us.

Before I can say anything, Tara speaks up, "She had another vision yesterday when she relaxed with Dr. Jennifer. She wasn't in a fight.

The Doc had Laden take her back to her room to rest. Only, she dreamed the whole scene again." Tara stops talking and looks around and lowers her voice. Everyone leans in to hear her. "Don't say anything to any doctors or staff, but she discovered that she can smell things, touch things and people, walk around, and the best thing is that she can have a conversation with the people in her vision. She found out when and how the ceiling collapse is going to happen. Isn't that cool? The only problem is that somehow these visions affected her eyes. She says they're better than they were yesterday. I can't imagine you looking worse. Sorry, that was rude."

Everyone at the table is smiling. But Jessy is the one who does the talking. "I think your eyes will go back to normal soon. Being able to talk to people in a vision and everything else that you can do now... is awesome! You might want to keep that a secret though. We can all do more than we're telling them. For some reason, all of us get a sick feeling when we try to tell the doctors anything. Did you feel like that too?"

I nod my head. "Yeah it's weird. My stomach flips around so much that I can't talk until I decide not to say anything. It's not with everyone though." I can't say anything about

Laden and I even though my stomach isn't what's telling me not to, my conscience is. I don't want him to get fired. "I mean, I can tell you guys and nothing happens."

Sherri cuts in, "Yeah, we'll have to fill you in on everything that we all can do another time when prying ears are out of range, if you know what I mean." She looks towards people at the table next to us.

Both of my morning classes cause havoc because everyone wants to get a good look at me. Minor chaos ensues. A few people even took pictures of me with their phones. Everyone wants to know why I look like this and what my vision was about.

After lunch, Todd and I leave the mess hall earlier than usual because he wants to take a more scenic route to Concentration Class. He says that the walk will do us both some good. I can't argue with that since I'm still a little stiff from all that sleeping.

While walking down a corridor together, I notice there are no other students anywhere to be seen. I really don't think this is the way to class. Where has he taken me?

Todd says, "Laura, I like you. I think we can be really good friends, maybe more than friends."

Todd stops walking and spins me around to face him. I feel warm and tingly all over, sort of nervous. He pulls me close to him and presses his hot, soft lips on mine. My heart starts to pound and I know I should stop this but I just don't want to. His lips are a perfect fit to mine.

Again an extremely hot guy is kissing me. Who knows why this keeps happening, right now, I don't care. OhmyGod he's such a good kisser!

I throw my arms around his neck. Our mouths, in complete sync with each other, are kissing in the most perfectly orchestrated way. Our movements coincide flawlessly with one another's somehow.

His body presses against mine and he wraps his arms around my waist. Without even the slightest stumble or awkward flinch, Todd opens a door and moves both of us into the room. My back is against a cold wall. His huge hand is on the side of my face holding my lips to his. His other hand is on my waist holding me to him.

I want him so much. I can't stop myself, not that I want to right now. My body needs him, wants to feel him. His firmness is pressing into me. His cold hands find their way under my shirt and under my bra. Twinges of passion shoot through my body awakening my most secret desires.

Why am I doing this? I'm not like this. I should stop, but I don't want to.

His lips leave mine and he drops to one knee pulling me onto the other. My legs straddle over his thigh. I'm still facing him with his lips glues to mine. His hand grabs my butt and he pulls me against him. He's so much stronger than I ever imagined him to be. His other hand is under my shirt caressing my bare back. His lips kiss my neck, softly, sensually.

I open my eyes and realize for the first time that we're in a janitor's closet. There are cleaning chemicals and toilet paper on the shelves and a mop and bucket right next to us.

As though my mind and body snap back into my control, I jump up off of his leg and back up against the wall. "You did it again. You jerk! You promised you wouldn't do that to me anymore. Are you that desperate for a girlfriend that you have to use emotional control just to get some?" I am really angry. I try to put my clothes back together again while he slowly stands up.

He looks confused and hurt, like I emotionally bruised him. "I didn't use it at first. You wanted to kiss me back and you did. You had full control of yourself up until we got into this room. Only then did I use a little persuasion but it was only to heighten your senses, not make you do anything that you didn't want to. I thought you'd like that."

"You didn't control me?" I'm having a hard time trying to think back and ask myself if I really did have full control of myself. Did I really want him that badly? OhmyGod! First Laden and now Todd... I'm turning into one of those slutty girls that I really despise.

"No, you asked me not to. You said not to ever take control of you unless you wanted me to, and I do really think at one point you absolutely did, so I amplified your senses. I really didn't have to push very much desire into you. That was almost all you and me babe." He smiles ear to ear.

"Yeah well... I'm... not... ready for a relationship right now. Everything in my life is already confusing enough. The last thing I need is a guy hanging all over me. So... well, you know..." Realizing that I'm probably hurting his feelings by saying that, I stop tucking in my shirt and look up at him. I should probably explain better. "Besides, I already have a boyfriend. At least, I had a boyfriend before I came here. He sort of broke up with me in an email recently. I'm not looking for a rebound guy."

"He might be scared of your abilities. Most 'normal people' fear the unknown, and well, we definitely fit into the unknown category that's for sure." Todd rolls his eyes and giggles a bit.

I lean out the door and look down the corridor to make sure there is nobody to catch us coming out of the closet together. When I'm sure the coast is clear, I take Todd's hand and pull him out with me, then let go as soon as we're out.

We start walking quickly down the hall to class. "Todd, I must say, that was really hot! I mean, we fit together like a jigsaw puzzle. You know?" I just know that I'm going to regret saying that one day.

Note to self: Stay the hell away from Todd when we're alone!

CHAPTER

THIRTEEN

After dinner we all pile into Todd's room in our pajamas so we can discuss the extent of each other's talents where no prying ears can hear. We all sit on the floor in a circle with a heaping pile of junk food and pop in the center of us.

Sherri starts it all off. "The staff here all know that if I touch someone I can see what they see and feel what they feeling, right? Well, there's more to it than that." She looks over at me. "Everyone here, in this room, knows that there's more to our talents than just what everyone else knows, so tonight, we'll fill you in on everything."

"You're going to love this." Jessy's smiling at me.

"I don't actually have to touch you to read you. I can read you from across the room. It's really hard and energy draining. I have to really concentrate on it, but I can do it. I'm getting better at it and it's tiring me out less each time I do it. However, if I do touch you, I automatically read you. I still can't stop that. I can also see some of the things you've seen and done recently. If I am touching you then I see it so much clearer and with more detail. So like I can tell you what colour of underwear that you put on this morning without touching you because I can see what you've seen. As of yet, when not touching you, I can only go back a few hours in your memory, but it's still really cool. I'm looking back farther and farther every time I practice. I can sift through your brain and pick out information that you know. Let me tell you, people do some freaky shit when they are alone." Sherri's giggling, probably remembering a reading where she saw someone do something weird.

"What's so funny? Fill us in." Todd questions Sherri but she just waves her hand and shakes her head no.

Sherri continues, "Most of the staff are too afraid to let me touch them. They don't want me to read them. It's like they all have a big secret... strange. Weird part is that I can't pluck it out of their minds. So whatever they're hiding... they're hiding very well."

"We all think there's something going on around here. We can feel it." Jessy takes a big drink of pop, and shuffles closer to tell his abilities. "Ok Laura, you are the only one who doesn't know the extent of my gift, and I would love it if you would take a ride with me." He winks at me and jogs his eyebrows.

I can't stop staring at him. What does he mean about take a ride with him? Please don't let there be another guy that likes me... I'm having a really hard time saying no lately.

"Don't look so worried, I'm not hitting on you." Jessy and the others all giggle, except for Todd who also let out a sigh of relief right along with me. "You already know that I can hold time, or speed myself up, however you want to look at it. Well, I've been learning so much more lately. I can now take people along with me. If I hold your hand, the world will slow down or stop around us. Or maybe we'll just speed up and the rest of the world goes super slow. I'm not really sure yet. Oh, I can also hold time for up to fifteen minutes now and getting lengthier every day. So, I will have to take you for a ride-along. Are you busy for about a half of a second... literally?" Everyone giggles including me.

"Nope, not busy at all. Besides, we're running low on pop. Can we make it to the mess hall and back before you're ability stops or exhaust you?" I'm really looking forward to trying this out. After all, isn't it everyone's dream to at least once in their life to stop time?

Jessy and I stand up. "Ok, peeps, see you in a second." We both laugh and he reaches out and takes my hand.

I feel a slight suction in the air and then, just like he said, the world stops. I look down at Todd who was tossing peanuts up into the air to catch them in his mouth and the peanut is actually stuck in the air... just hanging out there defying gravity.

Meanwhile, Jessy is watching my every reaction and smiling like a proud peacock. "Cool huh?! Come on, let's start walking. Oh and we are definitely going to change that peanut to a gummy bear. Todd hates gummy bears. If we can't mess with our friends, who can we mess with?"

After passing unmoving people in the corridors, we make it to the mess hall and load up with pop and gummy bears. Jessy takes a chocolate cupcake with lots of icing on it and smiles at me wickedly. He's up to something.

I roll the pops up in my shirt because we can't let go of each other's hands. We are on our way back when Jessy starts talking again, more seriously this time. "Laura, if you ever need to talk, about anything, just call me and

I'll be there in a flash, haha. Seriously though, I'm here for you."

We walk up to one of the frozen people in the hallway and he dips his finger into the cupcake, making sure he gets a good wad of chocolate and rubs the icing on the person's cheek. It looks like they didn't aim very well when they were eating chocolate. He does it to three other people. It's mean but hilarious.

"There are not too many people you should trust around here, even some people that you think are trustworthy, but you can trust me. I know how hard it is to adjust to being here and being kind of a freak, like we all are in our own way. You seem like a nice girl... the kind of girl that one should respect."

I know there is some hidden meaning behind what he just said but I don't want to assume anything. "What do you mean by respect? Don't be shy. Just say what you want to say."

Jessy holds his breath for a second before he speaks. "Ok look... I know that you and Todd have something going on and I think you should know that he's not the nicest guy around. I think you deserve someone who'll respect you more and not just want to... use you. You know what I mean. He has been a real sleazy guy to some girls. He can be really nice sometimes but not all the time, if you know what I mean."

How can he possibly know about Todd and me? "I don't know what you mean... me and Todd?"

"You left your full water bottle in the mess hall today so I figured with my speediness that I would run it to you before you got to your class. I ran the normal route and couldn't find you so I went another way. When I was walking down that corridor, I saw the two of you locked in a rather intimate embrace, so I hid and unfroze time. I don't know why I did that, it was wrong. I shouldn't spy. I'm sorry. I saw the two of you go into the closet together, hot and heavy. I, um, just want to make sure you know that Todd uses his ability on girls all the time. You are not the first, and you won't be the last. When he gets what he wants, he'll move on." Jessy looks very apologetic and sincere. I'm honored that he feels the need to protect me.

We arrive at Todd's door and I still haven't said anything to ease his worry, until now. "We didn't do anything but kissing, I stopped it. He said that he didn't really use much of his ability. I don't know why I..." I stop talking. What else is there to say? Thankfully, he doesn't know about Laden too!

Jessy gives me a shy little smile, "I just thought you should know. Oh and I didn't tell anybody. It's not their business."

With that said, he opens the door and we walk back through. He swaps out the peanut for a gummy bear, rubs a little chocolate on Todd's face and unfreezes time. Todd's face when he bites into that candy is priceless. He whips the half chewed gummy at Jessy who can't stop laughing. Everyone else is laughing so hard at the chocolate smeared on his face that Todd hasn't realized is even there yet. Jessy is just sitting back, eating the cupcake and laughing, trying to look innocent.

Tara laughs at Todd too. "So Laura how was it? Pretty wild, huh?" I nod frantically. She continues, "So you know about Sherri and Jessy, so Reilly, you want to go next?"

Reilly sits up from his lounging position and takes a long chug of a Sprite then belches out a five second burp. "Oops, pardon me. Well I can do mind control as you already know. What you don't know is that with the mind control I can also make people forget things. Not only the things that I've made them do, but regular things like whether they put underwear on this morning or not. I can also make a whole room of people forget if they put their underwear on this morning, not only just one person anymore. I'm so much more powerful now. I never use my abilities on any of you guys. Of course you wouldn't know it if I did... but I don't." He does an evil laugh, jogs his eyebrows and lounges back against the bed.

Todd looks at me and says, "You already know what I can do, but I can also kill someone if I want to without ever touching them. I can control their body energy so well that I can send them so much anxiety that they have a heart attack. I can also physically heat them up so they actually boil their own body from the inside out. I haven't killed anyone if that's what you're thinking. But I do have that ability if I ever had to."

"Ok, so that just leaves me." Tara is all giddy, so anxious to tell her talents. "Laura, you already know that I can leave my body and go places but what you don't know yet is that I can touch things like you can during your visions. I can move things around but I haven't been able to master taking things back with me yet. But I'm working on it. Oh, the best thing is that I'm starting to be able to travel hundreds of miles. I don't like the being sucked back into my body part of it, but I do love the getting out part. I can go and see what your parents are up to if you want, maybe leave them a message."

"No, that'll just make me miss them more and scare the crap out of them." I have to change the subject before I cry. I miss my parents so much. "Does everyone know everything that I can do?"

"Everybody knows. What we were thinking is now that you can see visions in your sleep, then maybe you could try to just close your eyes and have a vision, if you want to." Tara is the one to speak on everyone's behalf but all stare at me and nod from time to time. "Like, maybe you can bring it on at will and you just don't know that you have that ability yet. You are still very new to all this and it took us a while to get to where we are."

What Tara is saying makes sense. Since they have all been able to extend their abilities, then I should be able to do it to. Why not... it can't hurt, well it could make my eyes worse but it's still worth finding out. "I'll try. The worse that happens is that I fail. But then I can try it again, then again. Maybe one day... who knows? Tomorrow though 'cause I'm exhausted still."

Once everyone is finished talking, the majority of the junk food is gone, and my belly is swooshing full of pop, Tara and I decide to head back to our rooms so we can try to get some school work done before class in the morning.

Instead of heading to her door, Tara follows me to mine. "Can I come in for a minute? I have to ask you if you can help me with something."

"Of course, come on in. I'll help if I can." I'll help Tara with anything. She's so good to me. She's been a better friend to me than Andrea ever was.

We walk into my room and I almost jump out of my skin. Laden is standing in my room, waiting for me. The look on his face is probably the same expression I have; Oh Oh!

"Hi Laura, Tara, Sorry I'm in your room without your permission but I wasn't sure if you were sleeping and I wanted to bring you those clean towels that you mentioned yesterday that you needed. If you were awake then I was going to go get my clipboard and get started with the nightly taking of vitals. I'll need to take yours as well Tara, so don't run away. By being here you can save me the trip. Unless you'd rather me just come to your room later on and do it there." I thought Laden came up with a pretty good excuse. Better than what I would have thought up but I suck at coming up with a lie when I'm under pressure.

143

"Well, I'll be heading back to my room in about half hour if you want to wait until then, but you are more than welcome to check me over here and get it over with." Tara doesn't even seem to think anything of Laden being in my room. She isn't even shocked or anything. Maybe he lets himself into everyone's rooms whenever he wants. I wonder.

Note to self: Ask Tara if the staff let themselves into our rooms often when we're not in them.

"Ok, I'll go get both clipboards. Back in a minute." Laden walks past us both and out the door.

"Is it ok if I use your bathroom?" Tara's already walking towards the bathroom so of course I nod, what am I going to say, 'no you can't because if you do you'll realize that Laden didn't actually bring me clean towels'. Well, I have to think of something to tell her when she questions. Oh I'm so bad at this!

Laden comes strolling back into my room and wraps the blue squeezy thing around my arm and begins pumping it up. He leans in and gives me a nice soft kiss. I swear that my heart skips a beat. He says, "I was hoping you'd come back alone. I

144

was going to tuck you in."

The bathroom door pops open and out bounces Tara. She sits on the edge of my bed waiting for Laden to take her vitals. "So Laden where have you been hiding lately? Usually you're always hanging around."

Laden's eyes leave mine but he doesn't look at Tare, instead his eyes seem to be shifty, like he's trying to come up with an answer. "I've been needed to help out in another area. We're short staffed right now."

"What area?" Tara's really being nosey

"Um, in the… in another section. I'm just not needed as much here so I'm helping out on other floors and stuff. More hours, more money." Laden seems a little nervous. My stomach is telling me something is wrong. Either that or I might puke from all the junk food I ate.

While Laden is taking Tara's vitals, I go to the bathroom and thankfully, Laden actually had brought clean towels. That man sure does think ahead.

When I come out of the bathroom, Laden doesn't say a whole lot, he just finishes taking Tara's vitals and leaves.

She throws herself back on my bed and says, "OhmyGod that man is so damn hot! One night with him and I'd be ruined for any other man. How can one guy be that nice, that smart, and frickin' gorgeous beyond belief?"

"Oh yeah, he's definitely got the whole package. Have you ever tried to… you know… with Laden?" Oh if she only knew about him and me. I really want to tell her, but not just yet. "Has any girl that you know of?" Yeah, I'm being sneaky but I'm curious.

"No I never have. He's way out of my league! I don't think there's been any other girl either." Tara looks at me straight faced and says, "Laura, I really like you. I know I can trust you because my stomach doesn't get all yucky when I think about telling you secrets. So, I want to try something but you have to help me do it."

"Yeah, of course. No problem. What would you like me to do?"

Tara is so happy that I agree to go along with whatever it is she's planning. "Well, at first, nothing, just watch me, make sure I'm ok. Let me explain; I'm going to lie down on your bed, and I'm going to travel. Do you remember the room that says Restricted on the door?"

I nod my head in complete understanding. "The one that I suggested you travel into… of course. You want to go in there. I am so in. Just tell me my role and we can get started whenever you're ready." I can't wait to find out what's behind that door.

Tara laughs, "Woohoo! I knew you were the right choice for this! Ok, so when I travel, my eyes open and roll around and flicker sometimes. Please don't be afraid of that. Second, I'll talk to you, telling you what I see. Your task is to write down anything I say that sounds relevant. And the most important part is that I'd like to try and take something out with me. You know, bring something back. So, when I wave both my hands at you, like I'm saying 'hi' or if I yell at you, then sit me up and I'll come back to you. Or at least, I should come back to you."

I'm so scared and excited at the same time. I pick up the paper and a pen and sit down on my computer chair that I pull up to the bed. It reminds me of when Laden sat like this with me and how it was so intense when we started making out. Focus!

Tara lies down on my bed and stretches her arms out by her sides and starts breathing really deep, long breaths. After a few minutes, her body shakes a little and then her breathing goes back to normal but her eyes start shifting and blinking. It's kind of creepy.

That's when she starts talking in a really low whisper. "I'm out. I'm almost at the

Restricted area... start writing. I see books, shelves with folders, hundreds of folders. There's a nurses station with one nurse. I'm passing the desk now. I see rooms, hospital rooms, glass walls lining the hallway. There are people in the beds. There are breathing tubes and IV's in the first person, man I think. The second room, across the hall, is a girl, long hair, blonde, no tubes, sleeping maybe, coma perhaps. She's not moving. In the third room is a girl, short brown hair, OhmyGod! It can't be. I'm going in to make sure. It's, it's... Mabel Whitson! She's here! They said she was someplace else! They lied! Why?!"

Mabel Whitson is the girl that Reilly was sort of dating for a while. But she didn't take the medicine and she went into a coma because of the pain. She has my talents. Dr. Turner had said that they moved her to another hospital.

Tara is so upset. She must have been close to Mabel. She's right though, why did they lie about her not being in this hospital? Why would they not let anyone visit her? What are they hiding?

Tara spoke again, "She just said my name! I wish I could talk to her. I think she knows I'm here. Dr. Turner is coming into the room. He's looking at her chart, now her eyes with a light. He's watching the computers that are hooked up to her. He looks confused. He's talking to her. He's saying, 'Mabel what do you see right now?' Mabel says, 'I miss Tara'. Doc says, 'Do you see Tara?' Mabel says, 'In my dreams.' The Doc is writing something down in the chart and shaking his head. He looks sad. Doc is saying, 'I wish you'd have just taken your medicine Mabel. I waited a long time to get a Seer like you. Even with all that work, I was never able to get one to turn out like you. But just between me and you, I do have another girl, just like you. She's a brand new resident. She's a little older than you but her gift is still in its infancy stage. I must have patience. All in due time. She will have so much power because she is a natural. She is very special. If she only knew what she was capable of. I wish I could stow her away. Now don't tell anybody our little secret.' Doc is leaving the room. I am alone with Mabel. A nurse is coming! I have her file, pull me out. Hurry up!" Tara waves her hands frantically.

I grab Tara by the shoulders and sit her up really fast and start shaking her. She gasps loudly, "Ok, I'm back, I'm back, stop!" She runs to my bathroom and hurls, rather loudly I might add.

I look down in amazement to see that she brought the folder back with her. "Tara, you did it! You actually did it!" I smile and laugh. I truly didn't think it was possible, but here it is.

"Holy Shit!!" Tara's face is lit up with excitement. She starts flipping through the pages. She stops about two pages in and asks me, "Was Doc Turner your pediatrician from birth?"

"Yeah, from the day I was born. Why?"

Tara looks angry, "Because, he was Mabel's pediatrician from birth too. And he was mine. And he was Todd's. I need to ask Sherri, Jessy and Reilly if he was also theirs. There must be a reason why all of us had the same doctor all of our lives. It can't be just a coincidence. I bet he has something to do with all this!"

I say, "Maybe that's why Doc always told me that I was really special and very unique. He always says that I'm one of a kind. Now I know why he used to say that. How could he have known back then that I'd develop an ability?"

CHAPTER

FOURTEEN

We read through Mabel's chart and Tara heads back to her room. There's really nothing we can do tonight. Tara is completely drained from her travel. It took a lot of energy for her to grab that chart and bring it back with her. I still can't figure it out. It's scientifically impossible, right? I mean things like that only happen in the movies.

I fire off an email to my parents letting them know that I'm doing well and everything's great over here. There's no need for worry.

My mom writes back almost instantly, saying that she and dad are coming for a visit tomorrow. It's all set up. They'll be here just after breakfast. I miss them so much.

I shut down my computer and take a quick shower. I'm all tucked in bed and was almost asleep when... someone starts knocking on my door. Its 11:37 pm, on a school night. I get out of bed and open the door. It's Laden.

"Hi, were you asleep?" I don't think Laden cares if I was sleeping or not because he just comes in. "Is it ok if I come in?" His big glowing white smile is leading the way. The door swings shut behind him.

He walks past me then stops a few feet away. I stand there for a moment wondering if I should ask him to leave, only because my heart is pounding so fast. I could just say that I'm really tired. I decide to just go with it for now but if I feel threatened, I'll ask him to leave using some stupid excuse.

I start walking back to my bed. Laden grabs me around my waist from behind and spins me around. His lips press into mine. His arms hold me tight. I wrap my arms around his neck, holding his face to mine.

While still holding my waist, he walks me backwards to my bed. Laden lays me down with him on top of me. His movements are so smooth and graceful.

Even though I'm utterly exhausted, he is totally turning me on. I've never had a guy take control over me so gently and yet so firmly before. My other boyfriend dulls in comparison.

Laden kisses down my neck. He coddles my breast in his hand over my nightgown. He is so sensual that his kisses and his body movements are arousing me in ways I've never felt before... I feel sexy.

He starts sliding my nightgown up. Goosebumps follow his hand as it slowly glides up the side of my hip, along my waist and finally rests on my bare breast. He slowly kisses down my body.

Laden kisses me in places I've never been kissed before. My body is on fire, burning hotter than it ever has. I lose myself in his touch, his kiss. He loves me in an amazing way. I don't know for how long... time is irrelevant.

He kisses back up along my neck, to my lips. "Has anyone ever kissed you like that before?" I shake my head no. I cannot form words no matter how hard I try. Laden smiles his stunning smile and says, "I have to go now. Will you miss me?" Again I nod my head and he gives me another very sexy smile.

Laden stands up from my bed, and adjusts himself before turning to leave. He stops. Something on my desk captures his attention.

"Why do you have this?" I've never heard Laden sounds so angry. Even with a fierce expression, he's exquisitely handsome.

"I found it... on a bench... in a corridor." I have to lie. My stomach isn't giving me a queasy feeling but trusting my body right now, after the excitement it just went through, no way. So I lie... not very well either. "Why? I mean, it's just a folder. It's probably really old. I'll put it back tomorrow."

"You shouldn't have this. Do you know what will happen to you if they found out? I have to bring this back, right now. I know where it comes from but I have no idea how you got it and don't want to. You did not get it from a bench. Does anybody else know that you have this? Have you read it?" Laden's throwing questions at me but not giving me time to answer him. He sounds so serious, so worried.

"Maybe, yeah." I stand up from the bed but my legs are so weak that they barely hold me and Laden reaches out to steady me. For a quick moment, I'd swear that I saw him snicker. "Something is going on here. All the kids feel it, not just me. There's some big secret that I have to find the answer to. Maybe I'll get an explanation as to why we're all like this. Someone knows something. Do you... know something? Are you hiding anything from me?"

Laden kisses my lips softly and turns to walk out the door but stops. He tucks Mabel Whitson's file under his shirt. "Don't let any staff know that you know about Mabel... for your own safety, and now mine. Tell whoever knows about this file to keep quiet about it. I won't tell anyone about you." He pauses for a few seconds. "I only know that Mabel is there and that I'm not to tell anyone." Then he walks out the door.

If I wasn't worried before, I am now. I lie down in my bed, pull the covers up over me and look towards my door wondering if I should lock it. I decide that I'm too tired to get up and if someone wanted to get me, it wouldn't be hard, locked door or not. The keys are at the nurses' station anyway. After all, Laden did say that he wouldn't tell them about me knowing anything.

What did he mean about 'them'? Who is 'them'? My eyes, unable to hold themselves open any longer, slam shut.

Colours are swirling around me overtaking the blackness that was there a moment ago. Dammit, I'm starting another vision and I can't make it stop. The bubble starts moving towards me, closer and closer until I am completely engulfed. I'm forced to go through it. Where am I? I'm in a room with white paint on the walls. This is a hospital room. I'm so tired, why do I have to do this now?

The chart next to a bed has 'Mabel Whitson' written on it. She's waking up. Her eyes open and she looks straight at me. "Help me, Laura, please! Take me out of here. I can't run away. They'll stop me if I try. The drugs are so powerful. I can't help myself. Be very careful."

I wish I could just pick her up and take her out of here, to save her, but I can't. "What can I do? How can I help you? Give me as much information as you can. Quickly, please!"

Mabel lifts her weak arm and points to the room next to hers. "You will be there. Be careful. You can't escape once you're here."

"Who is keeping you here?" I wish she tells me.

"He didn't know any better and now there's no choice. It's in the medicine." She whispers so softly then closes her eyes. She drifts off to sleep.

I will myself to the room next to hers, scared of what I might see. There's no way that I'll end up here, no way. I see a girl lying in the bed, flat on her back. She's crying. She's me. OhmyGod! I'm seeing myself in a hospital bed. Ok, stay calm, don't freak out.

As relaxed as I can, I ask myself, "How did we get here?"

"In a vision." My crying self turns her head and starts sobbing even harder. "Help us. Combine for truth and justice."

Suddenly I'm being sucked backwards. My eyes pop open and I sit up in my bed. My eyes, they hurt, even to blink. They're burning.

I hop out of bed and rush to the bathroom only to stop for a second before I flip on the light. What will I look like now? My eyes were still red from the last sleep-induced vision. How bad will it be now? If they appear how they feel, they're going to be ugly. I prepare myself.

I flip the switch. I can't see anything but blinding light and redness. The light burns slightly less as my eyes adjust but the red is still there. It's like looking through a red film. I peer into the mirror and my knees get weak. I thought that I looked like a monster before? It's so much worse now.

Although everything's red I can still see clearly which is hard to believe when I look at my eyes in the mirror. The eyeballs themselves look like they're going to burst from all the blood that's in them. I think every blood vessel has ruptured. The blue in my eyes is now a bright purple. My lids, both the top and bottom, are swollen and also purple. I totally look like I was in a fight with an MMA fighter and I was too stupid to tap out.

I go back to get my phone and check the time. It's just past 6:30 AM. As fast as I can, I text 'I need to talk to you. I'm coming over' to Tara. Then I slip on my slippers and head for her room.

CHAPTER

FIFTEEN

Tara is standing at her door, holding it open, waiting for me. I run across the hall and into her room.

Tara grabs me and looks into my swollen eyes. "OhmyGod! Are you ok? Can you see? You had another vision... Tell me what you saw while I get you a cold washcloth for your eyes. Lay down."

I flop down on her bed. It's still warm from Tara's body heat. I must have woken her up with my text. "I saw Mabel. At least, I'm pretty sure it was Mabel since I don't really know what she looks like."

Tara puts the cold, damp washcloth on my eyes and even though it feels so good, I pull it off. Tara runs over to a cabinet and flings open the door. She pulls out her iPod and starts flipping through it.

I keep on explaining. "That's what was written on the chart, the same chart that we already read. Her exact words to me were, 'You will be there. Be careful. You can't escape once you're here'. And she pointed to the room next to hers. I asked her who was keeping her there and she said 'He didn't know any better and now there's no choice. It's in the medicine'. Then she went to sleep."

Tara flips the iPod around so that the screen is facing me. "Is this who you saw?" I nod my head, yes. "Then that was Mabel alright. I saw her yesterday too. She looked so skinny and sick." She motions for me to put the cool cloth back on my eyes. I do just that, I don't want to suffer the wrath of Tara.

I continue explaining, "I went to the room she pointed to and it was me in the bed. I was crying. I looked... paralyzed. I asked myself how we got there and she said 'in a vision'. Then she said 'help us. Combine for the truth and justice'. Then she started crying alligator tears. What do you think it all means."

"I think it means that we better hurry up and figure all this stuff out. We'd better fill everybody in, and fast. I'll text everyone and get them here a.s.a.p." Tara starts typing away on her phone.

"Ok, I'm going to run back to my room and get dressed real quick. I'll be back in five minutes." I rush back across the hall into my room and get dressed as quickly as possible. No time for a shower this morning, just brush my teeth and throw my hair in a ponytail then sprint back to Tara's room. Even though I'm rushing, I can't help but think about last night with Laden.

Just as I reach her door, Sherri is running down the hall with her book bag, trying to ponytail her out-of-control hair at the same time. I hold the door for her and let it go behind us. Before it has a chance to close Todd comes strutting in like he owns the place.

"Ok, we're only waiting on Reilly and Jessy. Everyone just grab a seat anywhere." Tara says as she's coming out of her bathroom. She's dressed now with her hair also in a ponytail. She's handing out little bottles of apple juice taking out an extra two bottles for the still missing guys.

Just as she sits down, Reilly and Jessy come through the door laughing about something. They plop down on the floor and accept the bottles of juice from Tara. Everyone is really quiet, tired looking and silent.

I guess I'm supposed to be explaining everything because everyone's staring at me. It's either that they're waiting for me to talk or they're staring at my haunting eyes.

Tara saves the day and starts telling everyone what's happened and how it all started. "Ok, last night I went back to Laura's room and I purposely drifted. I went through the Restricted door. When I drifted past the nurses' station and a shitload of files, I saw someone lying in a bed." She looks over at Reilly and says, "I saw Mabel."

Nobody says anything. They just look at Tara, confused. Even Reilly looks unsure of what she just said but a little angry too.

"Mabel's here?" Is all Reilly says.

Tara starts to choke up so I go on to explain, "Yeah, she's in there. She's not able to move on her own, we don't know why. But Mabel did see Tara. Doc Turner has something to do with all this. Tara saw him telling her about me, saying that he has a new girl that will have so much power because she's a natural and that she's very special. If she only knew what she was capable of. She doesn't know how powerful she is yet. If he is talking about me then he's right, I don't know the extent of my abilities."

I pause for a moment. Nobody says anything until Todd breaks the silence. "Why can't Mabel move? Is she drugged up?"

"We don't know." I continue telling them what I do know. "When Tara came back she brought Mabel's chart with her... somehow."

Tara adds, "Yeah it was so cool... anyways, we both read the chart and something popped out at us. Was everyone here in the care of Doc Turner their whole lives? Like from the day of your birth?"

Everyone nods yes, just like Tara and I thought. I say, "We were all cared for by him. He has something to do with this, but we don't know what, not yet anyway."

I'm trying to figure out an excuse as to why Laden was in my room and took the chart. It has to be good because Tara is going to question why he came back after she left. I haven't told her yet. No time like the present!

"Tara, after you left last night, Laden came back to check on my eyes." Now everyone's looking at me with one of those 'Sure-he-did' kinds of looks. I can't help but look at Todd, he's hurt. I can see it in his eyes. He knows that I betrayed him, no matter how much I try to lie. It's written all over my face, not only from the blushing but because I'm a terrible liar.

I have to get over this part of the story and tell everyone the rest of it. "He saw Mabel's chart on my desk. He freaked out. He told me to tell you all not to let any staff find out that we know something's wrong here. He was kind of scared. He said that now that he knows about us knowing, he might be in danger too. Anyway, he took her chart, hid it under his shirt and said he was going to try to sneak it back there."

Sherri suddenly gasps and points at me. At first I have no idea why she's doing that but then realize... she must have just read me. I remember that she said she's learning how to read people without even touching them. I'm pretty she just read me. I shake my head no at her with a look saying 'please-do-not-say-anything-about-it'! She doesn't, thankfully.

Note to self: Thank Sherri for not blabbing!

Everyone is curiously looking at Sherri waiting for her to tell them something interesting that she just read from me but look disappointed when she doesn't.

Todd is still looking at me with his pain ridden face. Unlike the others, he really doesn't want to hear what Sherri has to say.

He says, "So he knows something then. Did you ask him to tell you everything? Did he tell you or was he too preoccupied doing something or should I say someone?" Everyone can hear the anger in Todd's voice.

"I asked but he wouldn't say anything. I'm going to drill him about it next time I see him." I look at Todd, who looks like he's about to cry. I think I broke his heart. Damn!

Todd smirks, "Are you sure that he's not going to drill you?"

I shake my head no. Now is not the time to deal with Todd's jealousy, I have to continue. "After he left I went to sleep. I had a vision." I went on to explain my vision, every detail of it.

Sherri sits up on her knees. I fear what she might say about Laden and me. "So what you're saying is that we have to figure out why they're keeping her there and why they're lying about it. And why she can't leave. They must be keeping her prisoner for some reason. We have to get her out of there." Good, she didn't spill it.

Jessy put his hand on Sherri's shoulder to try and calm her down but Sherri jerks away, she doesn't like to be touched because it causes forced readings. Jessy looks apologetic then says, "We will, don't worry. We'll take one step at a time. We can't obviously go rushing in there. What scares me most is that you saw yourself there. We have to prevent that from happening, at all costs. Having one friend there is bad enough but two..." He shakes his head.

Reilly adds, "Yeah and we have to stick together, no matter what, like Laura says in the vision, 'combine for the truth and justice'. It must mean that if we somehow combine our abilities, we can straighten all this out. We just have to figure out how to do that and get my Mabel back to me."

Tara's looking like she doesn't really want to say what has to be said. "Laura, you're going to have to find out what Laden knows. He knows more than he's saying. Maybe he'll open up to you." She glances up at Todd whose eyes are now filling up with tears and her look changes to confusion.

Todd quickly stands up and walks into Tara's bathroom and shuts the door.

"What's up with Todd?" Jessy looks at me, then at Tara.

Tara, quick to answer, says, "I think he's sweet on Laura."

"I know that! So what if he is?" Jessy takes a second then flips his eyes up at me. He says, in one octave higher than his normal voice. "You and Laden? Are you two... really? How long has this been going on?"

Everyone looks at me then the bathroom door where Todd just went. Reilly bursts out laughing and says, "You and Todd too? Wow girl, you've been busy. And here I thought you were vanilla."

With that statement, I know exactly what everyone is thinking... SLUT!

Sherri comes to my defense, "Her being with Todd is Todd's fault. He really likes Laura, he actually respects her, maybe even loves her. He did control her some though. From what I saw, they only kissed but it was sexy as hell. Wow, I'm getting all turned on just viewing all this makin' out. Laden on the other hand is drawn to you for some reason. He can't stay away from you no matter how hard he tries. It's out of his control. Almost like a fat kid is drawn to an M&M. He can't help it. He truly, full on loves you girl. Ride it out girl or ride him, whatever." Everyone laughs except for Todd, who just rejoined us.

Reilly says, "Ok, let's stop torturing Todd. So now we just have to wait for Laura to get some information. Meanwhile, we all have to keep our eyes and ears open. Just be careful that nobody realizes what we're doing."

Todd starts walking towards the door and swings it open. "If we're done here, I'd like to go have breakfast before classes start."

That is our cue to leave. Todd's had enough, so we pack up and head down to eat.

I shake my head, raise and lower my shoulders several times which makes me look nervous. It's not far from the truth. I can't think of an answer to give him, except the truth and I don't think it's any of their business.

I ask, "Um, please don't tell anyone outside of this room ok? He can get into a lot of trouble, maybe even lose his career and I will probably get kicked out of here too."

Sherri looks at me. "Now I'm sorry that I don't read you more often. I try not to read you guys, but while in Rome..." She's quiet for a few seconds then says, "Wow... damn. They're hookin' up but they haven't gone all the way. Still, mm mm mmm he is smokin' hot and that man knows what he's doing. He has real talent. Not selfish at all."

I just know that she read me and saw things that have happened between Laden and I, including last night. My face must be as red as my eyes. She's still looking at me grinning like a fool. I can't help but give a nervous giggle.

Tara snickers, "I can't believe you didn't tell me. How did you keep that a secret? And for how long? That's why he was in your room. It wasn't for the damn towels. Well, I gotta admit, Sherri's right, he is smokin' hot!" Tara looks almost proud of me. She's a strange girl. In a whisper that only I can hear and pointing toward Todd, she asks, "So what's happened with him? Anything good and juicy? You'd better spill it girl!"

I whisper back so that no one can hear me, "Just… later, ok?"

Todd, with his eyes a little glossy and red, gains his composure. "So what's the next step then?"

Jessy says, "Laura is going to have to use her connection with Laden to get information. Do you think he'll tell you anything?"

"Um, I don't know. He seemed really scared about something, like if he told me anything, than he could get into trouble. I'll try my best." I can feel Todd glaring at me. My heart starts pounding and my body temperature rises really fast. Sweat is building on my forehead. "Todd stop it! I'm sorry!" I feel like such a shmuck. Even though I deserve whatever he does to me, he stops anyway.

CHAPTER

SIXTEEN

I almost forgot that my parents are coming this morning. With all the commotion, my mind has been preoccupied. I almost gobble through breakfast so that I can head to the main entrance and wait for them to arrive. I miss them terribly.

I'm overwhelmed with this intense feeling of sexiness. Not desire, but I feel sexy. I recognize almost right away that it's Todd's doing. I yell his name loud enough that he can hear me from around Tara. Immediately it stops.

Todd apologizes, "Sorry, I was just thinking and it got away from me. I'll try not to do that again."

Several minutes later, passion, sex, ultimate pleasure blasts into me. Without realizing that I'm even doing it, I let out a couple of moans from deep within me. Tara looks over at me and sees what's happening to me. She hauls off and punches Todd in the arm so hard that he yelps. Instantly the feeling is gone.

I hop up out of my chair and lean over Todd and whisper in his ear. "If you ever do anything like that to me again, I will tell all the girls that go to this school that you are done in ten seconds and that you don't come in an adult size. Do you understand what I'm saying to you?"

Todd nods his head. "Oops! I'm sorry, I slipped. It really won't happen again. I... promise." When I don't move right away, he turns his face toward me and whispers, "I promise that I won't do it again unless you ask for it or we're in a heated embrace and the moment calls for it. I won't promise that it won't happen again because it might. You might want it to."

"I won't... I really won't." I back up from Todd and walk back to my chair to get my stuff.

I pick up my sweater and say goodbye to everyone. I rush off to wait for my parents. A little time alone to relax before they get here sounds like a great idea. Everything that happened within the last twelve hours is whipping through my thoughts; Mabel, her chart, Laden, Laden and me, Todd... I just want my mom.

I sit on the bench just inside the glass doors and wait patiently. It's really quiet here. The plants are gorgeous. A tree that's two stories tall stands next to the window. The leaves are all on the tree. It's unusual to see a tree with leaves at this time of year.

Ginger Adams is opening the door to the front office when she sees me sitting there. "Well hello there Laura. How are you getting along here at Salvation? Are there any problems? Anything I should know about?"

Isn't that a hell of a question? What do I tell her? Oh Ginger, everything's great, my nurse and I are getting it on and I've also played with Todd. I'm turning into a total sleaze. Thanks so much for bringing me here. But of course I can't tell her any of that. "Everything's good, no problems. I like it here. My new friends are great. I've learned so much already."

She says, "Your eyes look pretty painful. Are they ok?"

I answer, "Yeah, they are sore but I had a vision and they get red sometimes when I do. I'm trying to figure out how to stop this from happening. However, if this keeps up, I'll be blind in a matter of a week." I giggle and shake my head. I'm joking of course, trying to lighten her worry.

Ginger doesn't laugh. She just smiles worriedly and says, "Well, I hope you figure something out soon. If you ever need anything, I'm here. Have fun with your folks. That's them there isn't it?"

I spin my head around to look. Sure enough, it's them walking up the sidewalk. My mom sees me first and starts running to the doors. I fling it open and she runs in, followed by my dad.

My mom's face goes blank when she sees my red, swollen eyes. She yells, "OhmyGod! What happened to your eyes? Why are they so much worse than before?"

My dad says, "Good Lord! Are you ok? Can you see?"

I reassure them. "I'm fine. I can see perfectly well. I've been having some visions and dreams and, well, when I become conscious again, this is how I look. It's getting better." I'm not lying. It is fading away as the hours pass by. They seem to be healing at a quicker rate than a normal person would be.

I hug my mom and she hugs back squishing me. Forcibly I have to pull her off me so that I can hug my dad. He squishes me too.

"I missed you guys so much." I say.

"Oh, Babygirl, we missed you too." My mom has her arm around me again as we start walking into the office.

My dad says, "I thought this hospital is supposed to be helping you adjust to your visions. It doesn't appear that it's getting any easier."

"Dad, it is getting better, I promise. I'm still learning how to manipulate my visions and because of that, I make mistakes and my eyes get all... icky. I'm ok." I try to make my parents understand and hope that they just drop it.

My mom gives me a questionable look to see if I'm telling the truth. When I don't flinch, she says, "Ok, we'll let it go, for now. If we ever see them worse than this, we're going to have words with Dr. Turner. Not happy words either."

I roll my eyes and slide the sign in book over to her. "You have to sign in. It's a stupid rule." I tell my parents.

My parents sign in and say the 'hello, how are you' greeting to Ginger. They start jammering on. My mom is quite the talker once she gets started. My dad puts his arm around me and gives me the look of 'here we go again, she won't stop talking'.

We make it back to my room where they hand me a gift bag. Inside is a cute little white babydolls pajama set, the ones that have the frilly shirt and the cute puffy panties. There's also some soft pink socks. In the bottom of the bag is a wide variety of junk food including chips, chocolate bars, gummy bears, licorice and random other stuff. I thank them so much.

I take my parents for a tour of the facility in the areas I've been told that I can take them; the residence where the kid's rooms are, including mine obviously, the mess hall and the classrooms. Otherwise, we're not supposed to bring them anywhere else, like the teacher's offices or the basement where the specially equipped rooms are where the kids can go to practice some of their more physical abilities, like setting fires, etc.

We end our tour in the mess hall where we sit and eat a small sundae. Well, mom and I do, dad has a coffee.

My dad says, "This is a really nice place. I didn't think it would be so much like an apartment building, only nicer."

Mom cuts him off. "Oh and it's so well decorated and pleasant. I'm very comfortable here."

My dad cuts my mom off to finish his thought. "The people all seem nice. Do you like it here Laura, honestly because if you don't, we will pack up your room and take you home right now?"

I smile and shake my head. "No, dad, I love it here. I've never been happier. Everyone is so supportive. Anytime, day or night, there's always someone available to help me out with any problem or concern. The teachers are more like older brothers and sisters than teachers. My friends are amazing. This place is so great. They actually take the time to listen to me and understand me, so I return the kindness. It's fantastic here. No offence, but I don't want to go home, not yet. I'm learning so much about my abilities and about who I am." I pause for a few seconds and smile. "I'm happy."

My parents and I go back to my room. It's almost time for them to go. Mom is sitting on my bed with me and my dad is sitting on my computer chair. I'm telling them about my friends and their abilities, not the full extent of their abilities of course.

There's a tap tap on my door then it opens slightly and I hear, "Laura, it's me, Jessy. Are you decent?"

I yell out, "Yeah, come on in."

He pushes the door open and bounces in. "Hello Sweetie." He stops when he sees my parents sitting here. "Oh, I'm sorry. I didn't know you had company. This must be your mom. You look just like her. Now I know where your beauty comes from. And this must be dad." Jessy sticks out his hand towards my dad for a shake.

My dad says, "So who might you be?"

Jessy says, "Oh, my name is Jessy. I'm a friend of Laura's. I'm a Holder." He pauses for a few seconds. "Oh goodness, I'm sorry. You probably don't know what that is. I can hold time still and freeze everyone. It's really neat. I play tricks on Todd all the time. The other day, he was tossing a peanut into his mouth so I froze time and switched it for something he really hates, a gummy bear. He was pretty upset but it sure was funny. I'm really talking a lot, sorry."

Mom smiles and says, "Well Jessy, it's very nice to meet you and no, you're not talking too much. Your ability sounds pretty fun. Sometimes I wish I could do that."

I ask Jessy, "Did you want something?"

Jessy answers, "No, no, it's not important. Lunch doesn't start for another twenty minutes so I was just seeing if you were here and wanted to burn up some time chatting. Not a big deal." He looks at my parents. "Will you be joining us for lunch?"

My dad stands up. "We've been here annoying poor Laura for way too long now and I think we should head out."

Mom stands up too and picks up her purse. "You don't have to walk us down. Stay here with Jessy. We know the way out." She leans over and gives me a hug.

Jessy cuts in, "Actually, she does have to walk you to the doors. Outsiders, no offence, aren't allowed to walk the establishment unaccompanied. And you have to sign out before you leave." Jessy isn't trying to be rude, but it is the rule. I remember reading that somewhere.

"Ok, well let's go then." Mom ushers everyone out the door.

Jessy and I get my mom and dad signed out and they leave to go home. I'm sad and I missed them before they even left. It's worse now. Tears fill my eyes.

Jessy wraps his arm around my shoulder. "It was nice that you got to see them. You will see them again soon, I'm sure. Now let's go get ourselves something to eat. We can chat along the way."

I wipe the few tears that fall from my red eyes. My tears are not clear. They have a red tinge to them. It must be because all the blood in my eyes is leaking out. I wipe them away with a tissue that was stuffed in my purse. "I know… it's just hard to see them leave."

Jessy, still trying to console me says, "I know Honey. Are you ok now?" I nod my head. "That's good. Can we talk a little bit?"

"Yeah, about what?" Oh, oh, here it comes. He's going to question me about Todd and Laden. I just know it.

After taking a deep breath, Jessy starts, "Don't think that I'm judging you because I never will. Ok, so if I have this right... you had a fling with Todd, then you had a fling with Laden, but you didn't have sex with Laden. Is that right? Do I have it down?"

I'm so embarrassed but if I don't explain it, he'll assume the worst. "Well, sort of. I had a make-out thing with Laden first, but we didn't do anything major. Then something happened, I lost my mind or I don't know... I ended up making out with Todd. It was really hot and heavy, but again, nothing serious happened. I absolutely did not want to do anything like that with Todd but that's how it turned out." I pause to take a deep breath. Maybe way deep down, I really did want to. No, I can't think that way. "But then, Laden and I, well, it got more serious. We haven't, you know, done it or anything. I like Laden, a lot. Can I tell you something?"

Jessy says, "I think I'm getting all of this straight now. I was a little confused. Thank you for laying it out for me. And you know that you can tell me anything sweetie. Of course it'll stay between us, that's a given."

I say, "Well, I feel like I'm being pulled at Laden somehow. I can't explain it but from the moment I met him, something really drew me in, like a magnet almost. I feel like I've known him a lot longer than I actually have. And Todd... well, I have a hard time being around him without wanting to be 'with' him, if you know what I mean. Why do I want both of these guys? I'm really not one of those kind of girls. I sort of dated only one guy for a few years. I wasn't with anyone else, I never two-timed him. He and I certainly didn't do anything other than kissing either. I'm a... well, I've never... you know. So, why am I being so hot and steamy with both of them?"

Jessy doesn't say anything for a moment. "Perhaps it has something to do with your ability. Maybe each of them has something to offer you that you don't know about yet. Or maybe you're just horny and need to get some." He smiles down at me and chuckles. "No but seriously, who do you want a relationship with, Laden or Todd?"

Without a moment's hesitation I say, "Laden."

"That was fast. Then I suggest that you stay away from Todd when there is nobody else around, that way you won't be seduced by his charming ways." Jessy pauses. "As for Laden, go for it Honey. He's a physically beautiful man and his character is unmatched. I think the two of you are a good fit."

He opens the door to the mess hall and we go get some lunch and sit at the table.

Lunch is typical and normal except that Todd keeps giving me the sad puppy dog eyes so I try to avoid looking at him. The rest of us act as though nothing's unusual. Like we aren't trying to save our friend and possibly every kid here at this hospital. We act like typical teenagers, laughing and tossing french fries across the table at one another.

Classes seem to drag on and on. All I can think about is how am I going to get information out of Laden when all I want to do when I'm with him is make-out. Thinking about last night and how he made me feel... I want him to do that again, and again, and again...

Concentration Class is lonely to say the least. Todd still stays in his typical spot beside me but he pulls his mat away from mine today. Through the whole class he uses his abilities to push despair, sadness and loneliness on me. I deserve it so I don't bother to tell him to stop. I think he appreciates it because his eyes meet mine after class is over and he gives me a friendly wink and a quick smile.

CHAPTER

SEVENTEEN

Classes are finally over for the day. I can go back to my room. Maybe Laden will show up and I can press him for more information. Or maybe we'll just make out. Butterflies start flapping around in my tummy. No, I have to get the information, that's most important. Stay focused. I try to make a promise to myself that I won't make out with him unless I get some info first but deep down, I know I'm not going to stick to that.

Note to self: Stay the hell off of Laden and get information.

I check my email account. None of my friends from the outside world are talking to me anymore except for Ronny but even he hasn't gotten back to me yet. How will they be when I finally do get to leave here? Will they accept me back with open arms like none of this ever happened? Will I even want to go back in their arms? Hell no! If they're treating me like this, then they can all piss off. I have new friends and they accept me fully and completely. I can't help but feel a little sad though.

Tara texts me to ask if my hot guy is here yet. I'm pretty sure she's referring to Laden. I text her back saying no. Almost a second after I send it, I hear a tap on my door.

"Come on in." I yell to the door.

Laden comes strutting into my room with a sexy grin on his face. OhmyGod! He takes my breath away, butterflies. I can't believe this incredibly hot guy wants me! I put my index finger up at him and tell him to hold on a second, then I text, 'guess who just walked in. Ttyl'.

Laden is standing in front of me with his hands in his pockets, wearing that amazing smile, looking absolutely delicious. I run my eyes up and down his body. I quiver. Damn he's impeccable!

I stand up and stroll over to him and run my finger over his lips, down his neck, down his chest, over his bellybutton and further. I can tell he's very happy to see me and getting happier every second. I throw my arms up around his neck and pull his head down to me. I start kissing him frantically.

He responds, kissing me back just as eagerly. Laden pulls me into his hot, hard body.

His abs and more are pressing into me. We somehow make it over to the bed. I spin him around so that I will be on top of him when we fall onto the bed. I end up sitting on him. We kiss with such passion that before I know it, my shirt is off and I'm wearing just my bra. His hands are on my thighs and he's pressing me into him.

Laden sits us up, and pulls off his shirt. I actually gasp. His chest is so smooth, sexy. The curves and ripples of his muscles make my body tingle in ways that make my toes curl. His skin feels so hot when our bare belly's touch. With me still stradling him, he starts kissing my neck. His arms wrap around my back, holding me against his delicious chest. My body, as though under its own command, is rocking back into him. Oh, yes! The passion, the excitement. I wrap my arms around his head as he breaths hard on my neck while he kisses.

In one quick, smooth motion, Laden flips me over. Now he's on top of me. My legs wrap around him tightly. OhmyGod this is hot! Laden is trying to undo my jeans when my 'Spidey Senses' tell me that someone is watching us. Oh please go away! Please, please, please!

I open my cycs and scan the room to try to find the source of my leeriness. Nobody, I can see nobody, but I still feel it. Then it dawns on me, we have an audience. Tara, Sherri, or both, are watching. Well that ruins the mood for me.

"We have to stop. I push on Laden's shoulders trying to lift him off of me but he's so strong. He holds on.

Still kissing my neck, Laden manages to say, "No, no we don't. We don't have to stop."

"Yes we do. We need to talk about last night." I give up on trying to lift him.

Laden gives an evil, sexy laugh and says, "Why don't you start describing what happened last night, in great detail, from the time I started kissing you, and I'll fill in the parts that might be foggy to you."

"Although that would be fun, that's not what I mean and you know it. We need to talk about what happened after the... fun... stuff." I just can't seem to find the right words to describe last night's activity.

Laden stops everything and lays still on me. With his face muffled in my pillow, he says, "Ok, but it's under protest. We can talk about the folder only if there's a possibility that we will continue from here later."

"I can promise that it's a possibility." I put it that way so that I'm not saying it's a definite.

I want to. With Laden... I want to but I'm a little scared. I've never done what we've done let alone go any farther.

Laden rolls off me and rearranges himself before he stands up. "Alright, what do you want to talk to me about... exactly?" He looks so serious, so much older.

With his chest still bare, it's really hard to keep myself from reaching out and touching his tight abs. I find myself staring at him, biting my bottom lip and dreaming of touching him again. I have to snap out of it!

"The folder... and why Mabel and those other people are in the Restricted area." I pause for a few seconds while I rearrange myself and put my shirt back on. "Please just tell me what you know. Something is really wrong here, it has to do with us kids and I won't rest until I know what it is. So either you tell me or I start asking around."

He sits down on my computer chair and takes in a deep breath and lets it out slowly before he says anything. "What I've heard is that years ago Doc Turner was under orders to do certain experiments on babies. He was to follow their lives and report the outcomes of the experiments. He didn't want to do it but he had to for some reason, no one knows why. And before you ask, no I don't know who ordered him and I don't know exactly what was done to the babies." Laden takes a deep breath and exhales slowly. "As the babies grew up, since he stayed on as their doctor, it was easy for him to convince the parents to let them all live here to get help controlling their newly discovered afflictions. This way he could study them easier I guess. I don't know how much of it is true or if it's mostly just a rumor."

Laden starts pacing from my computer desk to my bathroom and back. "I was told that some of the kids developed really severe brain problems and ended up in a vegetative state. I also heard that some died. Again, I don't know if it's true. A few have become dangerous with their gifts and have to be contained, this I've witnessed firsthand. Mabel's pain did put her in a coma for about two months. When she came out of the coma, her abilities were so powerful that she had to be sedated that way she wouldn't hurt anyone. So that's why she has to stay locked away and continually drugged. If she has visitors, they would ask too many questions." Laden sits down on the chair and stares at me as though he is waiting for me to say something.

"I just need a minute to sort all of this information." My brain is swirling with questions. Laden knows more than I thought he did. "So Doc is the reason that we're all here. I knew it! Bastard! What about Mabel's parents? Do they think she's dead?"

Laden looks so sad. "No, they do visit from time to time. When they come, Mabel has to be heavily sedated so that they don't find out anything. She has to be completely incapacitated or she might use her mind to talk to them. We think she's developed that ability but we're not sure. She can't be allowed to use it... not until we figure out a way to keep her sane and in control of herself. Her parents still think she's in a coma."

"How out of control is she? I mean, if she were taken off the drugs, all the drugs, how would she be?"

Laden shook his head back and forth, "I don't know. No one knows. Something happened to her when she went into the coma. She's never been taken completely off the medication. Every time they try, she causes chaos. She starts controlling her surroundings. One time she smashed a nurse's face when she flung a stool at her because she was going to give her a shot. She threw the stool with her mind. She's so powerful... but dangerous, Laura. She's like a two year old behind the wheel of an eighteen wheeler. She can't control herself."

I feel really bad for Mabel and her family, but I have to be more worried about my own safety and everyone else's right now. "Ok, so if Doc Turner knew that I knew all of this, what would he do to me?"

Laden takes my hand in his and covers it with his other hand. So softly and gently and with so much lovingness, he says, "I don't know, and I don't want to find out either. Just leave it alone, please. I... I can't lose you." His eyes are getting glossy.

I put my other hand over his. "I promise, I will be careful, but I can't leave this alone. I'm sorry. We need to know the truth, the whole truth. There must be more to it, things that even you don't know." I let go of his hands and stand up. I start pacing the same trail he paced a few minutes ago. "Like, WHO ordered Doc Turner to do this to us and WHY? Why do they have so much power over him? Are we just some kind of experiment for some crazy government conspiracy? Are more babies being experimented on? Why are we here sharpening our abilities? Who's going to benefit from it?"

"I can't answer any of that. I just don't know." Laden stands up, wraps his arms around me and kisses my forehead. "If you promise not to ask anyone any questions or snoop around putting yourself at risk, I'll see what else I can find out."

I hold on to Laden tightly and rest my head against his chest. I feel so safe with him. He loosens his hug and looks down at me. I look up. He asks, "So, how did you get Mabel's chart and don't lie this time. By the way, you suck at lying."

"Yeah, I've never been able to lie very well. Someone took it, mentally. I can't tell you who or how. Well the how is still a huge question in my mind anyways. There's more to some of us kids than anyone else knows and they'd be really ticked at me if they knew that I was telling you any of this. For some reason our stomachs get a sick feeling when we try to tell anyone anything. It's weird but I don't have that feeling when I'm talking to you." That's so true and I didn't even notice until now. I'm not queasy.

Laden kisses my forehead again and pulls away from our hug. "I won't ask you to explain anything then, ok? I'll just do what I can to find out who is behind all of this. Just remember that you promised me you'd be good."

"I will do what I can to stay out of trouble." I know he knows that I'm sort of lying, I am terrible at it after all, but I gave this my best acting. I also have my fingers crossed behind my back. Yeah, I know, it's juvenile.

Laden winks at me. He turns and while walking out the door, says, "I'm off shift tonight, so I'll be back."

As soon as the door closes, I text everyone and tell them to meet up in Todd's room. I put my phone in my pocket and check my hair and eyes really quickly in the mirror then head off to tell my friends what I've found out.

I fill everyone in on what Laden told me. Reilly is the first to speak. "We have to get Mabel out of there and off that sedating medication." He looks up at each one of our faces. We probably look doubtful after he spoke his next words. "I know if I'm with her… she won't hurt me. I know she won't. I love her and she loves me. She'll see me through her turmoil, I can help her. We just have to figure out a way to break her out of there and where to keep her until she's totally off those horrible drugs."

We all want to do just that, but how? I could ask Laden to help us get her out of there, but he's even afraid of what she'll do if her medication is stopped. Therefore, asking Laden to help on this issue… out of the question.

Sherri breaks her silence, "I can't see any possible way that we can do that. I mean, we could use Jessy's speed to get her out if we're able find a way to get him in there along with Reilly, 'cause Reilly is strong and could carry her out. But where would we take her while she withdraws from the drugs. We will get her back, Reilly, it'll just have to wait until something changes and gives us the opportunity. You will have her and hold her again, one day."

Reilly's eyes build up with tears. He gets up and goes to the bathroom and shuts the door. We can all hear him sobbing. Who can blame him? I wish he'd come out of the bathroom so I can hold him. It might help a little. I feel like a part of me is breaking when I hear his crying.

We decide to wait and see what Laden finds out. So we all go down for dinner as though nothing is wrong.

CHAPTER

EIGHTEEN

During dinner, a Mexican menu tonight, we thought it'd be good to meet up at Todd's room at around seven o'clock to watch a movie. It's Reilly's pick. Everyone just wants a night off from thinking about saving the world, so to speak. We just want to be typical teenagers. Sherri says that she wants to pick up all the junk food and pop and bring it to the room for us. After some protest, everyone agrees to let her do it, since she's insisting.

We all head to our rooms to do some homework and take some time to ourselves to do our own thing. I change into my most comfy jammies before heading to Todd's for the movie. I want to sleep in my new babydolls that my folks brought me, but I can't wear those to Todd's room, they allow too much skin to show. I don't see a point in torturing the guy.

Everyone arrives on time and picks through the pile of chips and candy to find what they like. We choose our seats while Reilly picks an action movie. I try hard to contain my excitement… NOT! But there is junk food, pop and great friends. What could be better?

After the movie, we sit around and chat it up for a little bit then all separate and head out the door to go back to our rooms. Todd grabs my arm before I walk out the door and asks if he can talk to me privately for a minute.

Todd looks me in the eyes. He has the most gorgeous eyes. I get transfixed when I look into them. "Laura, I know that you're in a relationship with Laden but don't you think he's a little too old for you. I mean isn't he like 30 or something?"

I'm a little angry that he's sticking his nose where it doesn't belong. "No, Laden is 23 years old, and since I'm almost 19 that means he's only about 4 years older than me."

"I just want you to know that I, um..." Todd shifts his eyes down to the floor and chooses his words carefully. "I really like you. I don't know why, no matter how hard I try to not want you, I can't stop. I think that we can have something amazing between us and I don't mean sex. I'm not trying to overstep here, I just want you to know that I'm here... for you. It just has to be said so you're aware that if he leaves you, I'll be here."

It takes a lot of swallowing of the pride to say what he said. What do I say now? "Um... well... thank you. I like you too Todd. But if Laden and I did stop our relationship, I'm probably not going to want to fall into anyone's arms for quite a while."

"I can wait... as long as it takes. I can't seem to break away from you. I want you. So I'll just... wait." Todd smiles at me. "Ok, you can go. I just had to let you know that. Now that it's said, I feel better."

Great! He might feel better but I feel like a shmuck. Not only do I have Laden caring about me, I have Todd as well. Yup, I am one of those girls that I can't stand. Lovely!

"Well, um, thank you, again. I'm going to go now. I'll see you tomorrow at breakfast, ok?" With that said, I rush out the door before I decide to let my instincts take control and jump him.

I finally get back to my room and strip my clothes off and hop into the hot shower. Maybe the water will wash away my problems. If I could only be so lucky!

I put the water as hot as I can handle it then start shampooing and soaping. I stand right under the water and let it wash over my head and down my face. I stand like that for a long time while the water rinses the shampoo from my hair. I lather some cream rinse in it, pull it forward so that it's hanging down my chest and stand with the hot water flowing smoothly down my back. It feels so good like it's washing away all of my troubles.

"You look so sexy in there." Laden is in my bathroom... watching me!

"Why are you in my bathroom?" Even though I know that he can't really see through the shower door, I still try to cover up my private parts.

"I came back to see you, remember, I said that I would." Laden is taking off his clothes. I can kind of see him. "Can I come in with you? I'll wash your back."

Laden is naked. Butterflies are frantic in my belly. I can't make out any details of Laden's body but I can see his entire skin colour, no clothing hiding anything. He's coming towards the shower and me in it, naked! Nobody has seen me totally naked since I was a little girl. What if he doesn't like what he sees? OhmyGod! Do something Laura!

"I've never... I mean... wait... I'm scared." I roll my eyes because I can't believe I just said that.

Laden stops at the shower door and doesn't open it. "I will never hurt you. I will never do anything that you don't want me to do.

I don't want you to be scared, ever. I'll wait until you're ready. Is it ok if I still watch you shower? You look so sexy in there! I can't see anything clearly but I can watch your general shape, and I love what I see."

"Um, yeah, that's ok." I only have to rinse out of my hair to be finished but if it turns him on to watch me, and I know he will never hurt me, then why not.

I take my time rinsing out my hair. I can feel his eyes on me. It's turning me on and I'm pretty sure it's probably turning him on too. Everything turns him on. I giggle but I don't think it's loud enough for Laden to hear me.

I turn the water off and open the door, just a little. "Can you hand me a towel?" There is no way that I'm coming out of this shower stall naked with him staring at me. No way.

Laden picks up a big fluffy white towel and hands it to me. I notice that he also has a white towel wrapped around his waist and nothing else on. My stomach is doing the butterfly thing again.

I dry myself off and wrap the towel around me and take a deep breath. I open the shower door and step out. My legs are shaking. I really hope they hold me up. How humiliating would that be?

"You are so beautiful." Laden is looking straight into my reddish eyes and smiling just a little smile.

Good Lord he is gorgeous! His calves are strong and formed like a bicyclists are. His chest draws my attention, entrancing me. There's something about his chest that fills me with desire. It's so rippled, so strong that I want to run my fingers up and down it. Kiss all of it. His arms are so manly, strong and thick, not like a guy my age. Of course his face is magazine perfect with that drop dead gorgeous smile of his.

I still can't believe he likes me, my stomach flutters fiercely. Damn butterflies go away!

He takes my hand and walks me to my computer chair and sits me down. He then goes back to the bathroom and returns a few seconds later with a towel, a brush and my hairdryer. He plugs in the hairdryer and sets it down long enough to towel dry my hair. Laden tirelessly blow dries it and carefully, painlessly brushes the knots out afterwards.

He puts his hands on my shoulders and gently guides me over to the bed and sits me down. He lights two candles then turns out the light. My stomach is flipping around so much that I might puke.

I am ready for this. I want Laden to be my first. I love him. I'm just nervous as hell. I take a few deep breaths nonchalantly so he doesn't notice my anxiety.

Laden kneels down on the floor in from of me. "If you would prefer, we can just watch TV." I shake my head no. Laden has the softest expression on his face. He smiles adoringly at me. "I will stop anytime if you ask me to."

And with that said, I lean in and kiss him. His gentleness is so reassuring. His patience is admirable. His touch is so gentle. Laden is making this a magical, memorable night. It is beautiful. He's beautiful.

Candlelight is softly reflecting off of our glistening skin. The sounds of our rhythmic breathing, so erotic. The sweet saltiness of his skin. The scent of passion in the air. So much time is passing but nothing outside of us and this room exists. At least… not tonight.

CHAPTER

NINETEEN

I wake up to the sound of a ping from my phone, a text message. As the sleepy fog slowly leaves me and I try to lean over to get my phone, I see a beautiful man lying next to me in my bed. How could I have forgotten?

His breathing is soft, slow. I find the rise and fall of his chest is soothing to me. His face, relaxed, flawless. I could just lay here and stare at him all day. At this exact moment I feel like the luckiest girl in the world. Do I deserve to have a man this exquisite beside me? I must because he's here.

Trying not to wake him, I stretch to get the phone before it beeps again. Sure enough, it's Tara, 'So how was last night? Is he as gorgeous naked as I think he is?'

I text her back using only one hand. 'I'm looking at him right now and yes, he's perfect!' and hit the send button. I try not to giggle when I picture how the expression on her face must look. I bet her mouth is hanging open right now.

I slip out of bed as carefully as I can and head for the bathroom. I have to try and look presentable. He can't see me with a glistening oily face, hair all knotted up, terrible breath and leftover residual mascara smeared down covering my still slightly purple bags and blood red eyes. And I have to pee. My eyes look much better today than they did even last night.

Quietly, I open the bathroom door and tiptoe my way back to the bed. I lift the covers and slide in next to him. I want to wake him up nicely. I tickle my fingers down his chest ever so lightly, just barely touching him. The tiny hairs lift with my touch leaving goose bumps trailing my fingers.

"Good morning." Laden speaks in his non-whispering voice and makes me jump and screech. He starts laughing. "I've been awake for a while. I watched your sexy ass while you tiptoed your way to the bathroom."

"Why didn't you say anything?" Seeing me naked last night in the candlelight mixed with all the passion is one thing, but in the morning when there is light peeking out from behind the drapes?! My face must look like a tomato because I sure can feel the heat.

"Baby please don't be embarrassed. Your body is beautiful, perfect in every way because it's yours. I love looking at you. If you have a flaw anywhere on you that I wouldn't like, I haven't found it. Even if your body was covered in old scars it wouldn't matter to me. I see you, not your body." His eyes stare deep into mine making me gasp.

Laden shifts himself so that he's propped up on one elbow. He slides the covers down exposing my body to the slivers of sunlight. I'm a little embarrassed and feeling quite exposed. In my mind I keep telling myself to relax, that it's ok because it's Laden looking, nobody else.

"Absolute perfection." Laden runs his warm hand up and down my body several times then hops out of bed quickly. "Give me a minute." He struts his perfectly sculpted body to the bathroom.

My eyes are locked on him mesmerized by his every movement. He is so flawless, like he was sculpted from clay by a very gifted artist. He is utterly captivating, so perfect. I don't think that even after a hundred years, I'll ever really understand what he sees in me.

I pull the covers back up over myself and roll onto my side and start to giggle. That amazing man made love to me last night for the first time… my first time. That sexy, gorgeous, fabulous man made love to me!

To top off a perfect evening, I had a dreamless night. I just realized that I didn't dream about anything. I slept soundly. I don't have good nights like that very often anymore so I appreciate when I do. Perhaps it was due to Laden being here. Maybe we can do a little experiment and have him stay over again, just to see if it works.

The details of last night fill my mind and I lose myself in the memory of how gentle he was. He made me feel so at ease. I wasn't self-conscious at all last night, not once. I felt only love, his love, pure and real. We joined into one; our movements, our breath, our touches... exceptional, beautiful.

Butterflies flap in my belly when he slides into bed behind me, cradling my body against his. "Do you have any regrets about last night?"

"No, not at all. Actually the whole experience was better than I had imagined it would be... because it was with you." I feel a tear roll slowly down me cheek. "You were so sensitive and caring. You made it an amazing night to remember. No regrets, not one." I want him to know how perfect it was for me. I can't find the exact words to fully make him understand.

"I'm falling in love with you." Laden whispers in my ear and starts kissing my neck.

I whisper, "I think I'm falling in love with you too." He's falling in love with me! Butterflies!

To break up what was just about to be the most fabulous morning I've ever had, there was a tap tap on my door. The wake up reminder knock that the staff give us on school days.

Laden fly's off of me and sprints in two steps to the bathroom, out of anyone's direct line of vision from the door. His eyes are huge and he's breathing fast, shallow breaths, but quietly, very quietly.

I bust out laughing because the look on his face is priceless. He thought someone was coming in and that he needed to hide. Quickly!

"It's not funny. If anyone saw me here, with you, I would lose my job, my career. I can't be seen sleeping with a patient!" Laden is genuinely scared.

My laughter continues. "I've never seen you move so fast. You almost flew. Are you sure you don't have an ability to fly? I'm sorry but it was so funny."

We have a quick shower together, get dressed and then he slips out of my room, hopefully unnoticed. I grab my backpack and head over to Tara's room so that we can walk together down to breakfast. I'm sure she must have some questions for me.

Just before my knuckles meet her door, it fly's open and she grabs my arm and yanks me inside and lets the door shut behind me.

"OhmyGod! So tell me all about it. Is the rest of him just as perfect as his face?" Tara is talking so fast. "Tell me, tell me, tell me!"

"Yeah! He's... exquisite. It was an experience that I will look back on very fondly." I left out the part about us telling each other that we're falling in love, that's just between him and me.

"Tell me more. Was he romantic or wild? Tell me, tell me!" Tara is actually bouncing up and down with eyes huge and a smile from ear to ear.

"Romantic, so very romantic. Candles... a gentle touch. The whole night was so... paradisiacal. That's the best way to describe last night." I pick up Tara's backpack and hand it to her. "We're going to be late for breakfast. Let's go."

She looks at me questioningly. "Ok, so what does paradisca... paradisle... whatever, mean?"

I start to walk out the door with her following closely behind me. "Paradisiacal. It means; of or like paradise. Basically the entire experience couldn't have been better if I dreamed it up."

She doesn't push for much more information but she does ask, "So are we going to tell the crew that you and Laden..." She drops her sentence because Todd comes around the corner.

Quickly and under my breath, I say, "No we're not saying anything." I give her a very stern look so she nods in agreement.

"G'morning. Am I missing a good conversation? If so, fill me in." Todd seems extra happy this morning. I wonder why.

"No Todd, Laura and I were just talking girl talk. You wouldn't be interested." Tara shoots me a look to say 'there are you happy, I didn't say anything'.

We eat breakfast and head off to our classes. Sherri has an early appointment with Dr. Jennifer so she isn't here this morning. I am so thankful that she isn't going to read me right now. I'm not ready for the looks that she'll give me or what she might say.

Tara keeps pressing for more information all through English. I simply refuse to tell her any of the details of last night. I want to keep the magic just between Laden and me. It feels like, if I tell her everything, it will lessen the experience somehow.

After English, Tara and I separate while she heads off to her scheduled visit with Dr. Jennifer and I head off to Concentration Class.

Butterflies flutter in my belly. Am I going to be able to suppress my excitement from last night away from Todd? I really don't want him to pick up on it. I don't think I can bear to see the pain he'll show in his eyes.

Todd and I are lying side by side on our own mats and trying to concentrate on the new relaxation technique that Maria has just explained to us.

Todd turns his head towards me and whispers, "I'm glad that your first experience was pleasurable for you."

I spin my head around and look like a deer caught in a headlight. How the hell does he know?!

"I just wish it would've been me. But since it wasn't, I'm glad he didn't hurt you. At least he made it nice for you." Todd whispers.

His expression says 'brokenhearted' but it says 'friendship and love' as well. He's keeping his emotions from travelling over to me so I can't really tell what he's feeling. Of all the times for him to not share his abilities with me, I wish this wasn't one of them.

I take his hand, intertwining our fingers and give him a friendly 'thank you' smile. We hold hands through the rest of the class and all I feel coming from him is a relaxed calm. I do all I can to hide how elated I truly am about Laden. It wouldn't be right to show that emotion to Todd. I'd feel like I was rubbing it in.

After class I walk around looking for Laden. Usually he's walking the halls busy doing something. But today, he's nowhere to be seen. I give up looking and head to the mess hall for lunch.

I'm the first to the table. Slowly they start to trickle in; Tara first, then Reilly and Todd. Then Jessy shows up a few minutes later.

Reilly says to me, "Laura, your eyes are looking better. They're not quite as red, and the puffiness has calmed down. You're looking good. You have a nice glow today."

I respond, "Thank you. I slept well last night, no dreams." I smile a quick smile and turn my head so he doesn't see the pink flush that I know is all over my cheeks.

When Sherri comes to the table, she puts down her tray, sits and puts her hand on my arm. Immediately her face goes blank. At first I have no idea why she's touching my arm, then it hits me... she's reading me in depth. She'll know everything that happened last night as if she were there in my body.

By the time I yank my arm away, it's too late. She's grinning from ear to ear. She knows everything. I give her my best 'please-do-not-say-anything-about-it' look, but she's not looking at me.

"Oh, that was fantastic. Wow! Damn! Skills! That man has him some skills! Mm mm mmm. Is it getting hot in here?" Sherri starts fanning herself. Her face is flushed and her forehead is starting to glisten. She has a look like she's in heaven, kind of what I must have looked like last night. "I knew something was up with you. You radiate satisfaction. I can feel it in every fiber of my being."

Tara laughs her best 'OhmyGod-so-it's-true he is awesome' laugh. I can't help but smile through my embarrassment. My face feels like a red hot pepper. So now the cats out of the bag or at least, it will be when Sherri spills it which should be at any second.

Reilly and Jessy are just looking at us wondering what it is that they're missing. They're probably waiting for one of us to fill them in on the big funny. Sherri is fanning herself, enjoying the afterglow and Tara is still laughing at Sherri's reaction.

Todd on the other hand, just looks miserable. To him, knowing that Laden and I had a great night is one thing, but for everyone to know that I am officially Laden's girl, body and soul, is too much. His eyes well up with tears. He clears his throat fighting back the lump and says to Reilly and Jessy, "Laden spent last night with Laura." The way he says it sounds kind of matter-of-factly, like, pass the salt. I think he'll break if he allows himself to feel any more emotion. He's trying to shut it off but he's failing miserably.

Reilly and Jessy both look at Todd. Jessy say, "Oh, sorry Todd." Then he looks at me and whispers. "Congratulations Laura." With a giant smile splashed all over his face.

Reilly pats Todd on the back. "Sorry man." Then goes right back to eating.

Todd is really quiet for the rest of the lunch hour, but so am I. Saying anything about last night will just hurt Todd more.

Thankfully Sherri held off on giving Tara the rundown but she did not stop looking at me and grinning huge while she read me even more, over and over again. Even though I want to stand up on the table and tell everyone how wonderful Laden is, I don't dare!

Back in my room, sitting at my computer, emailing my mom and dad, I keep looking at the bed, and smiling. It almost seems like a dream, like it never really happened. It was too perfect to be real. If I wasn't physically tender, I might just believe that it didn't happen.

I close my computer and flip on my TV. After flipping through every channel and not finding anything that interests me, I shut it off. My mind wanders back to last night.

Knock, knock on my door then it opens slowly. "Laura, you in here?" It's Laden. My guy, my love, the man I melted into last night. My belly flutters and a smile blooms on my face.

"Yeah, I'm here." I walk over to him as he's strutting to me. We meet and instantly we're in a passionate embrace, kissing and holding each other tightly. My arms are around his neck and my hand is combed into his hair holding his head down to me so I can kiss his soft lips. His arms are around me, holding me to him. His lips leave mine only for a moment to kiss my neck. I gasp to catch my breath. I'm almost losing myself completely, again.

Laden pushes me back at arm's length away from him but he's still hanging on to me. "Ok, ok, I'm still working. Oh, yummy girl!" He pulls me back to him and kisses me passionately again then pushes me away again, this time letting me go and stepping back. "I want to stay but I can't. I was just passing by and I thought I'd stop in, kiss you, and tell you that I'm being moved to the Restricted area for a little while. So, I'll snoop as much as I can. But, deliciously hot girl, I can come back later, around 9:30… if you'd like."

"Yes, please do! I'll be waiting for you, in my bed, naked at 9:30 tonight. You won't keep me waiting will you?" I slide my hands up his shirt and run my fingernails gently down his chest and belly. He loves it and responds accordingly. I'm teasing him and I like the affect it's having on him.

"Since you put it like that, how can I resist? I will not be late, promise." Laden kisses my lips softly one more time then flees back out my door.

I fall back onto my bed grinning ear to ear. I bury my face in the pillow that he laid his head on when he slept last night and breathe him in.

CHAPTER

TWENTY

I jump, scared at first. Then my sleepiness fades and Tara's face comes into focus. "Hi sleepy head. Are you coming down for dinner or do you want to sleep more? I texted you but you didn't write back. I was a little nervous about coming into your room. I thought that I might walk in on you and Laden doing... you know. Although seeing him naked is a huge fantasy of mine, I really don't care to see you naked."

"Ok, ok, I'm getting up. Just give me a minute." Trying to stop her from rambling on and on, I get up and go to the bathroom and close the door.

I catch myself all through dinner from losing myself in a stare. No matter how hard that I try not to, I can't stop thinking about Laden coming to my room tonight. The anticipation is wearing on me. I can't even suppress it for Todd's sake, I've tried. I know he feels it. I also know that he must be hurting and angry.

Sherri leans across the table and in a whisper she says, "I won't read you tonight but if it's anything like last night then I can't wait to read you tomorrow!" I shake my head and turn a lovely shade of red but smile a wicked sexy smile at her anyways. "Ooooo girl! You be like a cowgirl on a bucking bronco for me, ok?" I can't believe she said that.

The rest of our meal goes by somewhat normal except for the few looks that I'm get from Todd. I pretend that I don't notice, that way, maybe he'll quit trying to make me feel like an ass.

Before we leave the dinner table, I announce to everyone, "Expect a text from me tomorrow morning so that we can meet up before breakfast. I'll probably have more information." My eyes meet Todd's but I look away quickly. I can't bear to see the hurt in his eyes anymore.

Tara, Sherri and I hang out for a few hours after dinner. Sherri tells us about her first time with a guy. Her experience was pretty lousy, worse than Tara's. It was his first time too and it was over in about ten seconds, and it hurt, a lot. She says that she's never bothered to have a second time and has no interest unless she finds a man that is worthy of her body. She says that she's in no hurry.

Listening to that, I am really happy that Laden was my first. He knew exactly what he was doing. He was extremely gentle. Everything was perfect. He made the whole night very pleasurable for me. My happiness was what he was after, not just his own.

I look at the time and realize that Laden is going to be in my room in half hour and I promised that I'd be ready and naked for him. So I'd better prepare.

"Girls, I gotta go, he'll be in my room soon so I'd better be there too. Um, do me a favor Tara, no drifting in… Sherri, no reading tonight! Tara, that was not cool that time I felt you once before and don't try to deny it." I hop off Sherri's bed and head back to my room, a smile permanently glued on my face.

I grab a quick shower and light the candles then climb into my bed and wait for Laden. At 10:00 I'm up pacing from my desk to my bathroom and back. Where is he? I've texted him five times and he hasn't texted me back. If he's working still, he won't have his phone on him, I know that, but I keep trying anyways. He said that he'd be here. He has never gone back on a promise, not yet anyways.

Then it hit me like a brick and my heart sank, he went to the Restricted area to snoop around. What if they caught him? Would they keep him there against his will? I have to do something but what can I do. It's not like I can just go and knock on the Restricted door and ask for Laden.

I'll wait another fifteen minutes. He might just be working overtime. Maybe one of the patients had some kind of a horrible accident and they need his help. That must be it, I have to calm down.

By 10:30 I can't take it anymore. I text Tara and within seconds she's bursting through my door. I fill her in on what's happening. She immediately texts the rest of the group and tells them all to come to my room right now.

I realize that I'm only wearing my bathrobe and decide that it's probably best I put some clothes on before they all get here. I can hear people coming through my door asking questions in whispering voices before I am even out of the bathroom.

Tara fills everyone in on the situation while I go around blowing out the candles. Todd is leaning against the wall with his arms crossed obviously upset about the whole situation and not caring what might have happened to Laden.

Jessy who's already seated on the floor, looks up at Tara, "You have to drift to the Restricted area again. You have to at least zoom around and see if you can find him anywhere."

Sherri looks at Jessy then me. "He has a point. There's no sense in everyone getting all in an uproar just yet. Maybe Laden is just working overtime, I mean, people work overtime and sometimes can't get to a phone to call home. My dad used to be like that all the time."

Reilly chimes in too, "Yeah Laura, you said that he doesn't carry his phone on him when he's working, right? So he probably just hasn't had a chance to get to his phone and check his texts. Maybe he doesn't realize the time."

Todd sticks his two cents in as well. "Or maybe he's just an asshole and decided that since he already got what he wanted from Laura, he's done with her. Did anyone think of that?" Everyone glares at Todd. "Sorry, but we do have to consider that as a possible reason for the no-show."

Everyone turns and looks at me. "No way!" I look directly at Todd and figure that I'll just fire right back at him, hurt him like he's trying to hurt me. "After the amazing night we had last night, and with what I promised him for tonight, he'd be a fool not to come back. If it had of been you, wouldn't you come back tonight Todd?"

"I'd be here in a heartbeat and you know that. It would take me being dead to stop me from coming back to you. But that's just me. So... where is he?" Todd is just trying to hurt me now. I have to ignore him. There are more important things to deal with right now than his ego.

"Tara, do you think you're up to trying to drift tonight? I know that you're tired but this is important." I am really hoping that everyone can just shift their focus back to finding out what happened to Laden.

"Definitely! I'll do anything to get away from this tension." Tara says as she's flopping out on my bed and telling everyone to stay quiet with her shushes. "Laura, I'll need you to do what you did last time if I tell you to ok? Maybe if I wrap my arms and legs around him, I can not only bring him back, I can get a cheap thrill too." She winks at me. I know she's only joking around. She would never betray me like that... it's not in her nature.

I smile and nod, remembering that I'll have to shake her to bring her back. She closes her eyes and puts her arms at her sides.

Sherry quickly asks Tara "Is it ok if I latch on and watch what you see? I really want to see what's behind that locked door. I'll try not to drain your energy, I promise."

Tara nods so Sherri lies back on the floor and stretches out. With her having practiced her skills, she doesn't even have to touch Tara to be able to follow her. She just closes her eyes and somehow, she can see through Tara's eyes.

Tara begins her deep breathing. Todd, Reilly and Jessy are all staring at her waiting to see something happen. They're afraid to blink for fear that they might possibly miss seeing her soul levitate from her body or something. I want to giggle but I remember back to when I watched Tara do this for that first time, I don't think I blinked either.

A few minutes later Tara's body begins to vibrate then completely relaxes. Tara whispers and everyone except for Sherri, who's in her own trance, moves in closer to hear her. "I'm in the Restricted area. I don't see anyone. Not even a nurse at the nurses' station. I can see Mabel so I'm going in to try and talk to her."

Reilly moves as close to Tara as he can, desperate to feel closer to Mabel somehow. I whisper softly, careful not to wake up Tara or Sherri. "Reilly, don't touch Tara, it'll wake her up." I take Reilly's hand in mine, trying to comfort him. "You're going to hear her having a one sided conversation, she'll fill us in on what Mabel or anyone else says when she comes back."

Tara interrupts with her conversation with Mabel. "Mabel, wake up honey. Have you seen a male nurse called Laden?" A pause for about fifteen seconds then Tara continues, "So do you know where he is now?" Another pause… "Can you tell me what they were arguing about?" She pauses for a few seconds. "Did Doc Turner leave with Laden?"

My stomach feels like it just sank right out of my body. I can feel the blood leaving my face. So it's true? Doc Turner must have discovered Laden snooping. I must be squeezing Reilly's hand hard because he gives a quick squeeze back. I look at him and apologize. I blink away tears.

"Yes, Reilly knows where you are, I told him. We're all trying to figure out a way to get you out of here... He knows that, but I'll tell him anyway... What?! .. No, Laura is fine. She's not even in the room next door. I have to go, but I'll be back very soon, I promise." Tara's very quiet for a good long minute. "Laura, the room next to Mabel's is still empty. I'm going to keep looking around... I see Doc Turner! I'm going to go see what he's looking at. It's a folder for some new guy, I think. I've never heard of this kid. It says that he healed his broken femur in a matter of a few hours. Wow, that'd be cool."

Todd asks Reilly then Jessy if either of them knows of a kid who can heal himself but each of them shake their heads no.

"There is nobody else here." Tara's eyes are fluttering and looking around the room as though she's searching for something. "Laden is not here, anywhere. I've done all I can do. I'm coming back now."

I prepare myself to grab a hold of Tara's shoulders and start shaking her but I hold off. She told me only to do that if she asks me to. Instead I say, "Tara, Tara are you back? Come back Tara."

With a gasping breath, Tara flips her eyes open then runs from the bed to throw-up in the toilet.

"Does she always hurl after a drifting session?" Jessy is holding back a gag of his own from hearing Tara hurl.

I shrug my shoulders. "I think it depends on how fast she comes back to her body. I really don't know. We should ask her."

Sherri pops up from the floor with the biggest grin on her face. "OhmyGod! That was so cool! Now I know what it feels like to fly, to be totally weightless. Absolutely amazing!" Sherri's eyes meet Reilly's. She slides over to wrap her arms around him.

Immediately, Reilly's eyes filled with tears that soon fountain down his face onto Sherri's shirt. He swallows hard. "What did she say?"

Sherri, still smiling says, "She wants to tell you that she misses you, loves you and would never, ever hurt you." Tears are streaming down Reilly's face so Sherri hugs him again for longer this time.

Tara comes walking out of the bathroom looking really pale. "Laura, I looked all over in the Restricted area, but I couldn't find any sign of Laden. Sorry, I was hoping I'd see him." She comes over and sits on the bed to hold my hand, probably because I'm crying like a baby.

Pain! Sheer, agonizing pain! My head is going to explode. Remembering that the medicine Doc Turner prescribed me for the pain is in my backpack, I reach out to grab it, but fall face down on the floor. The last thing I remember seeing is Jessy trying to grab me on my way down. Then… blackness.

CHAPTER

TWENTY-ONE

The blackness seems to be staying for a long time. But without fail, the colours slowly start to creep up. I don't think I'll ever get used to seeing these amazing blends of rich beautiful hues. The bubble is slowly coming closer. It's getting bigger, sharper, more defined.

I step into the bubble and let it engulf me. I search around me for anything familiar but see nothing that I recognize. I'm standing on the side of the road, more like a highway. Cars are flying past me. My focus is drawn to one vehicle in particular as it speeds closer to me. I recognize it as being the van that brought me to this school.

I concentrate on the van and blink. When I reopen my eyes, I'm sitting in the backseat, next to a kid that I don't recognize. The boy is looking out the window and doesn't see me.

In the front passenger seat I see Ginger Adams, who's talking to the driver. She says, "I know that you have plans for 9:30, you won't have to cancel. We have lots of time."

The driver answers her back with a familiar voice, "I just want to make sure that I am back in plenty of time." I focus on the rear view mirror, the eyes in the mirror. It's Laden. Laden is driving the van. It's him that's talking about being back by 9:30.

Am I looking into the past? When my vision started, it was way past 9:30, so why am I seeing this now? I don't understand, the clock in the car reads 8:19. I'm confused.

In a flash, I'm sucked out of the van and standing on the side of the road again, looking at the van. A red car starts swerving back and forth across the road until it smashes into the side of the van, spinning it around in a circle. The red car flips onto its roof and slides down the road. The van spins sideways once more then also flips. It's rolling over and over again.

I'm screaming and running towards the it, hoping and begging that what I'm seeing is only my own imagination and not actually what's going to happen, or has happened already.

I finally reach the van, which is now rested onto its roof. I run right to the driver's side and get down on my hands and knees to look in through where the window once was.

Glass is all over the place and the steel roof is crinkled up like tin foil. Laden is upside-down still strapped in his seatbelt. His face has some cuts on it but otherwise he's alive. "Laden, are you ok?"

Laden looks at me, his eyes wide. "Laura? How the hell..? How did you get here?"

"My vision... I'm here through a vision. It's actually around 11:30, for me, so I guess I'm coming back in time. Can I help you get out of the van?"

Ginger's eyes are glued to me, big like saucers, "How are you here? Did your ability bring you here? Are you that powerful already? You are amazing."

"Hi Ginger, Are you alright?" I reached in to pull some glass away from her arm and she grabs my hand.

"I can actually touch you. This is fantastic." Ginger is smiling huge for someone who's just been in a rollover accident. "Can you see if Randal in the backseat is in one piece?"

I crawl to look in the backseat at Randal and almost throw-up. He is smashed up really bad. His face is full of blood and his arms look broken. Then I realize that he's not breathing. "I... I think he's dead."

Ginger says, "No Laura, Randal's ability prevents him from dying. He should be able to heal himself."

I crawl back to Laden who has undone his seat belt and is now crawling out of the window where the windshield used to be. I help him stand. Ginger is also crawling out.

"I have to go make sure the other driver is alright." With his arm around my shoulder to help steady him, we start walking towards the red car. "Do you know why you're here? If it's 11:30 in your time and you're back here..." Laden looks at his watch, "It's only 8:20 right now. You can't prevent the past. So I don't make it to you on time tonight, do I?" He looks really upset.

"No, we were looking for you. I thought they caught you snooping and did something to prevent you from coming to me. Why are you driving in this van tonight anyway?" Laden starts to get more steady on his feet as we walk down the highway to the little red car. Cars are stopped all over the road on both sides. People are everywhere.

"Doc Turner asked me to. I tried arguing with him and telling him that I had plans but he insisted. Bradley Rathem was ill today so admissions asked Doc if he could spare me so that I could assist Ginger in coming to pick up

Randal. I figured I'd be back in plenty of time to meet up with you for 9:30, so I didn't bother to call. By the way, sorry that I don't make it but at least now, you know why. Your eyes are a beautiful blue again, at least in your vision they're perfectly clear, I wonder why that is. Do you think I'll remember that you were here? If I don't remember, tell me about it. You'd better head back to your body. It's not good to be gone for so long. I'll catch up with you soon. I'll bring a washcloth for your eyes ok." With a laugh, he lets me go and walks away from me.

I close my eyes, take a deep breath and scream really loud so I can pull myself back to my body. With a great sucking feeling, I'm being pulled back fast through the bubble and past all of the swirling colours into the blackness. I like I'm spinning down through a funnel this time. It's not the same.

I'm stuck in the blackness, spinning and flipping around and around. I take another deep breath and scream again. Nothing… just blackness. I scream and scream and scream but it's not pulling me out. What do I do now?

CHAPTER

TWENTY-TWO

I stop screaming long enough to hear someone calling me. They sound so far away. I call out to them, yelling, "I'm over here! Please help me! I'm stuck in the blackness."

The voice is in front of me, softly speaking, "Laura, reach out and take my hand. I will pull you out, just take my hand."

I reach out blindly towards where the voice is coming from. My hand is flailing in front of me. "I can't find you. Where are you? Help me." I'm panicking, so scared.

"Laura, it's me Tara. I need you to calm down, take a deep breath, concentrate hard and then try again. Reach out and find my hand." Her voice is so calm.

I try really hard to calm down. I close my eyes and breathe deeply. When I feel relaxed, I reach forward and feel a hand. I intertwine my fingers with the ones in front of me then feel a hard tug then the hand let go.

I gasp and wake up back in my body again. Gasping for air and totally confused. I look around the room, looking for Tara. She was the one who came and pulled me out, so where is she? "Tara? Where are you?"

I feel so alone. Out of nowhere, Jessy appears, standing beside my bed holding my hand wearing his favorite dark blue sweater. "Laura, I'm here but I can't stay long. You're ok. We're going to get you out of here, we promise. Laden is going to come see you in a little while. You have to pretend that you are groggy, like you're drugged. Trust me. Tara is here with you in spirit. She's going to be coming and going, so if you need to get a message to us, just talk when nobody is around you. Hopefully Tara will be here to hear you. I have to go before I weaken and enable someone to maybe see me." Jessy kisses my forehead and in a streak of dark blue, he's gone.

I look around and I shudder. I realize where I am. Mabel predicted correctly, I'm in the glass room beside hers. I don't want to be here. I'm so scared.

A nurse comes walking into the room with a smile on her face and an ice pack in her hand. "Welcome back Laura. You were out for a few days. I'll put this ice on your eyes dear." The nurse fluffs my pillows and places the ice pack over my eyes. "Now you rest up. You've had a rather traumatic few days."

I feel a needle go into my shoulder and before I can flinch away, she pulls the needle out. I'm drifting into a sleep, but I don't want to sleep. My lids slam shut.

I awaken still groggy from the shot that the nurse gave me. How long was I sleeping? It's dark in here. There's enough light where I can still see but it must be the middle of the night.

I try to sit up but I'm so weak that I just can't. I want to go, just get up and walk out of here. My legs won't work right, they feel numb almost. I have an IV in my arm connected by a long tube that leads into two bags of fluid. One bag is big with clear fluid in it. The second bag is much smaller with a pinkish coloured fluid.

If I remember correctly, Reilly was here and he told me to just talk when nobody is around and maybe Tara will be here in spirit and she'll hear me.

Hoping she's here, I speak as loud as I can which is just a whisper. "Tara, are you here with me? I've never felt more alone. My legs are numb and my thoughts are foggy. I'm so tired. Why am I here? When is someone going to come and get me? You pulled me from the blackness when I was lost, but I'm not lost now, so it'll be easy. Please." My exhaustion takes over and I drift off to sleep again.

People are talking around me like as if I'm not here. I pretend that I'm still sleeping and listen in as best I can.

One man says, "So how strong do you think her ability is?"

I think I hear Doc Turner's voice say, "She's strong, but she is still discovering. She will be a powerful Seer once she fully develops her skills."

Another man's voice breaks in, "But is she the one we're looking for? Will she be able to do both, go back in time and ahead in time? Will she have the ability to, for instance, find an assassin and be able to physically be there strongly enough to kill him whether it's in the past or the future?"

Doc Turner replies, "Well, I don't know yet. I thought for sure that Mabel Whitson had that ability but her anger is so prevalent that I can't take her off of her medication long enough to test her. She's dangerous to the people around her, but I just don't know if she can project. I'm not sure if we'll ever know. As for Laura, I don't know."

The first man's voice rings out again, "When will this girl be ready for brainwave testing? We would like to have something to report back to him. Something positive… hopefully."

Doc Turner picks up my hand and holds it gently. "Her name is Laura. Please be so kind as to using her name when referring to her." Doc pauses for a second. "I will test her tonight. We will stop the medication now and test her in a few hours. If you would like to come back later I should have a full diagnosis for you then."

Man number one replies, "You'd better."

I hear rustling of clothing then it's just Doc Turner in the room with me. I can hear him moving around.

"Ok Laura, you can open your eyes for me dear. I know that you're awake. I'm going to stop the drugs that make you so groggy." Doc Turner pauses and lets out a big sigh, "I don't want this for you Laura, for any of you kids. You need to know that I have no choice. I had to inject them when they were born."

I open my eyes and look at the Doc. His eyes are filled with sadness, a look that I have never seen him wear before. I speak softly, "Who made you do this?"

Doc looks up at me and smiles, "I knew you were awake. Oh Laura, you know I can't tell you that. It's for your own safety."

"How did I get here?" I need some answers.

Doc Turner holds my hand again and explains, "You fell into a vision but you weren't coming out of it. I told you to take the medication that I gave you but you didn't and your vision overtook you, same as Mabel's vision overtook her. You were screaming and screaming but wouldn't wake up. Nurse Lorraine heard you and called us up to help. We had to bring you here to the hospital wing. We drugged you into an unconscious state when we realized that we couldn't stop your screaming. To stop your panic and to prevent your eyes from blinding, we had no choice but to drug you."

"I'm awake now, so why can't you let me go back to my own room?" I really want to go back to Laden's arms.

Doc Turner drops his head and sighs again. "I can't let you go now. They know you're here. They know of your ability. I just have to prove to them that you're talents are not as strong as they need them to be and that they never will be. The brainwave test that we're going to give you, once all of your mental awareness comes back, will prove to them that you're not what they want. Then maybe you can go back to your room."

"Doc, what if I can do what they want me to do? What will happen then?" I'm scared. I don't want anyone to take me away.

"Can you do what they need you to do? Has your ability matured that quickly? That's never happened before." Doc looks at me, almost afraid of what my answer might be.

I say to him, "I can. At least, I have. That's what got me here. I was looking for... someone. I went back in time. I got stuck in the blackness on my way to my body. Do you suppose I was lost?"

Doc walks a few steps from my bed and runs his hand over the few strands of hair he has left on his head. "I won't let them take you away. I promise. We'll figure something out."

Doc leaves the room without another word. It's so quiet that it's almost deafening. Tears start streaming down my face. I don't want anyone to steal me away. What am I going to do? A brainwave test cannot be tricked or faked, can it?

"Tara… Tara are you here?" A feeling like someone is watching me flows through the room. I know its Tara, I remember the feeling from when she did it once before. "I'm scared."

Suddenly I see a blur of blue and white. Standing beside my bed is Jessy and Todd.

They had been holding each other's hand. "Why were you two holding hands?"

"Don't you remember Laura? When we travelled together I had to hold your hand so I could bring you along." Jessy is smiling hugely. "I'm going to bring you into a time freeze with us so that we can stay with you longer with less risk of being seen."

Jessy and Todd hold hands again, with a grimace from Todd. Jessy holds my hand. A feeling of whirling lasts a few seconds and the world seems to stop.

Jessy says, "Laden has been a real help. He's been keeping tabs on you, like what medicine they're giving you, etc. Tara keeps coming and taking your chart so that when Laden's off shift and can't get here, he can still read it and explain all the medical mumble jumble to us. Then Tara brings it back. I bet you didn't know that she could do that, put things back where she gets them from, I mean."

Todd reaches out and touches my leg. "Tara was listening in when Doc Turner was just talking to you and she told us what he said. So Laden is going to try to be there when you go for that brainwave test tonight. Hopefully, they'll let him stay with you. We're hoping that with him there, you'll feel calmer." Todd sighs. "He really is a nice guy." Just saying that must be hard for Todd. Todd thinks of Laden as his competition. He's changed somehow.

"I'd like him there." Suddenly I remember. Laden was in a car wreck! "Is Laden ok? The car accident... I was there. Does he remember me being there?"

"He's fine Laura. A few cuts on his otherwise perfect face, but he's ok." Todd still seems a little jealous. "But yeah, he remembers you being there. He told us that you helped him. And you'll be happy to know that the kid that was in the backseat and Ginger are ok too."

"Tell Laden... tell him, I miss him." I can't tell Jessy or Todd to tell Laden that I love him. So I guess saying that I miss him will have to do.

Jessy looks around and nervously says, "Laura we have to go. The nurse will see us if we don't leave soon because I'm getting real tired and time is starting to tick again, slowly, but it's ticking. I can't hold it back much longer."

"Take me with you, please! Don't leave me here." I am begging.

"I can't. I'm not strong enough to take two people right now, and I don't even know if I could even if I were fully rested. I'll be back as soon as I can." Jessy kisses my forehead and moves aside without letting go of Todd or me.

Todd leans in and kisses my lips with a soft kiss. "Stay strong. I'll... we'll get you out of here."

In a split second Jessy releases my hand and a streak of blue and white disappears. I am alone again.

Through the glass wall I can see a nurse coming to my door. She's carrying a tray of food. "Hello, I'm Karen. I've been caring for you while you've been asleep, so-to-speak. Are you hungry 'cause I brought you a hamburger, fries and a pop? You must be famished, IV fluids aren't very filling." She smiles.

Karen is very tall and very thin. Her hair is short and deep red. She smiles a lot but doesn't show her teeth when she does.

She sets the food down on my table and swings it over in front of me then pushes the button on the bed so that it sits me up. She adjusts the pillows behind my back so that I don't fall over then picks up the TV remote and starts flipping through channels.

I hadn't even realized that a TV was in here. "Do you know who those men are that were here earlier?" I have to take a chance and ask her. Maybe she'll know.

"I'm not sure Honey. They only come when a new patient comes to the Restricted area of the hospital. I'm not sure what they're looking for but they must see something in you that they like. I overheard the one guy say that he thinks Mr. Stratler will be pleased with this one, meaning you, I suppose. I've never seen a Mr. Stratler." Karen tells me everything that she knows while she flips through channels on the TV. I'm sort of surprised that she's being so candid.

"My arms won't let my hands hold the burger. Why can't I move? Am I being drugged?" The burger smells so good. Pretty soon I'm just going to try to fall face down onto it so I can take a bite.

"Oh, here let me help you." Karen holds up the burger for me to take my first bite. "Yeah, they're giving you something so you can't leave. It's for everyone's safety. If Mabel hadn't been immobilized, she could have caused a lot of damage. We just have to make sure you're not dangerous to yourself or others. So until then, I'll be here to help you. If it were up to me, it would be different, but it's not."

"You're not afraid of me?" My words are barely understandable because I'm talking with a mouth full of french fries.

"Nah... I'm not scared." Karen smiles big and puts the straw up to my mouth so I can wash down my fries.

CHAPTER

TWENTY-THREE

I must have drifted off to sleep again after I ate because I didn't see Karen and Doc Turner come back into my room. They're taking off my covers when a gurney comes rolling in. Laden is pushing it. I want to jump up into his arms but I can't, first of all because physically I'm paralyzed and second because nobody is supposed to know about our affair. I'm so very happy that he's here, even if I can't touch him the way I'd like to.

"Ok Laura, are you ready to go for a ride?" Laden asks me with the biggest sexy, crooked smile. Even with little scars on his face from the rollover car accident, he's astonishingly handsome... he takes my breath away.

Laden wraps his arm under my shoulders and lifts me up while Karen holds me by my ankles. Without alerting anybody, Laden blows a kiss at me. The two of them lift and move me over to the gurney and set me down gently.

Karen throws a blanket over my body and tucks it in around my legs. Laden takes my IV and transfers it from the pole on my bed to the pole on the gurney.

Doc Turner speaks next. "We're taking you for that test I was telling you about earlier, do you remember?" I nod my head. "You don't have to do anything except relax and watch pictures on a TV screen while we measure your brainwaves. But first, electrodes are going to be stuck to your head with putty."

"Can Laden stay with me? I'm a little scared and I'll feel more comfortable it I have someone who's familiar to me come along." I'm desperate to have Laden with me for as long as he can be, even if we have to play along as just friends and never touch each other lovingly like I so desperately want to do.

Doc Turner looks at Laden questionably and returns his eyes to me. He smiles and says, "Sure, I can't see that as being a problem. During the test Laden, you won't be able to talk to her but you can perhaps hold her hand so that she knows you're still with her." Doc looks back at Laden, raises his eyebrows and shakes his head, in a not so approving way then lifts and drops his shoulders. "Oh well, it was bound to happen sooner or later."

Laden stays right by my side. It takes about half hour for someone to stick the electrodes on my head with gooey putty. Laden talks to me casually the whole time, never letting on to the nurse that we are lovers. I still feel slightly drugged and a little tired so my contribution to the conversation is very small.

They roll me into the room where the test is going to happen. There is a TV hanging in front of a weird looking machine that I've never seen before. Laden scoops me up and sets me down into a chair that looks like the dentist's chair. He seatbelts me in so I don't fall off since I've only regained enough usage of my left arm to allow me to lift it slowly. The rest of my body is still sleeping.

Over the speaker system I hear Doc Turner's voice. "Ok Laura, are you ready to begin?" I nod my head not sure if he can even see. "All you have to do is watch the screen in front of you and think about the pictures and movies that will be shown. No talking please. Let's get started."

The lights flick off and the screen lights up with pictures of people's faces. Then a series of odd photos and movies play out on the big TV screen. About half hour later the screen goes dark once again and the lights come back on. Nothing that I just witnessed is relevant to anything. Everything was random and therefore made absolutely no sense.

Doc Turner comes back on the speaker and says, "That's it Laura. You're all finished."

Laden gives my hand a little squeeze and stands up to pick me up and lay me back down on the gurney. "I'm going to pull these electrodes off then I'm going to wash your hair. It was looking really nasty before the putty so you can imagine how bad it looks now." He laughs as he starts yanking the electrodes off of my head one by one. It doesn't hurt because he's just pulling them out of the putty, not actually from my scalp.

"It'll feel so good to clean my hair. Even without touching it I can tell it's gross." My eyes meet his and for only a moment, we lose ourselves. "Thank you... for everything." I'm so glad that I have Laden in my life. Where would I be without him?

He pushes my gurney to a room where he can wash my hair. Doc made it a point to insist that Laden leave the door open since I do not have all of my strengths back because I'm still drugged. He's just looking out for me, like a dad would do.

After Laden lays me out on what I imagine is called a washing table, he starts setting the temperature of the water, gets the shampoo and conditioner and a soft fuzzy towel. The water feels so good washing down my head. Laden's hands are gently washing and scrubbing all the putty out of my hair. Why does this make me want him?

Laden leans over and kisses me softly. "I wish I could take your clothes off and wash your whole body down for you. Wouldn't that feel good? With you being unable to move, I can do anything I want to you, with your approval, of course... just a little fantasy play." He growls like a tiger then kisses me softly, slowly, again.

Once Laden finishes with my hair, he wheels me back into my glass room. Laden and Nurse Karen move me back onto my bed and she tucks me in nice and tightly again. Karen leaves the room but Laden stays, fussing with my pillows and IV. I think he was just stalling until she left.

"I want to lye next to your warm body and hold you while you sleep, keeping you safe. However, I'm going to leave for a while and get you some water and I'm also going to see if I can get a glimpse of the test results. Don't worry. I will be back, soon." Laden settles for squeezing my hand since no one should witness him kiss me, then leaves my room and heads off down the hallway.

I close my eyes hoping to fall asleep so that I won't dread the moments as they tick by until his return. I miss him already.

CHAPTER

TWENTY-FOUR

I wake up hearing voices yelling in the hallway. I can't see anybody but one of the voices belongs to Doc Turner. Several minutes pass by as the yelling continues. I hear three or four men walking down the hallway. Scuffing sounds from their dress shoes give them away.

Four men come into my room. Doc Turner and Nurse Karen follow right behind them. The light flicks on. One man walks up to my bed while the other men stay back. Nurse Karen stays next to the door but Doc Turner pushes past the men and comes to stand on the other side of my bed. He looks scared.

The man in the fancy, expensive suit standing next to my bed looks at me for what seems like ten minutes but is probably more like two. I'm not sure what he's looking for but he's looking straight into my eyes. I keep trying to look away from his leer but I am drawn back in disbelief of his rudeness.

I can't take the silence anymore. "Didn't you mom ever tell you that it's rude to stare at people? Who the hell are you?"

The man speaks, "I'm sorry, Laura, how rude of me. I'm Mr. Stratler. I don't mean to stare at you but I wasn't expecting you to look so... real. According to your test results, you can travel the world with just a simple desire to. You can travel back in time and change history. You single handedly can go back and stop the events of September 11th from every happening. Do you know that you have that kind of power?"

Mr. Stratler answers me with something I wasn't expecting. "To be totally honest, we want you. We need someone with your ability. Your world needs you. Many, many years of research and experimentation went into creating you, the perfect tool. We'll be taking you to our facility immediately so that you can be properly trained for what is your destiny. This is what you were created for Laura, so don't bother trying to fight us."

"What if I don't want to go with you? Like, do I even have a choice in this?" I'm starting to panic now. Where the hell is Laden?!

"Well no, you really don't have a choice. Think of it as a personal sacrifice for your country, your world, like being drafted. You will be coming with us, right now." Mr. Stratler turns to his cronies and waves them over.

Next thing I know, these men are picking me up and placing me down on a thinner gurney and strapping me down. I start screaming as loud as I can manage. I can't physically fight them off. One man stabs me with a needle and a burning sensation immediately follows.

My vision starts to get blurry. My screams dull down to mere whispers. Somebody help me! "Tara, I hope you can hear me. Please, help me!"

Seconds later, from the right side of the room, I can hear Tara. "I heard you call for me Laura. We're all here now." I turn my head and the room spins around me. I see Tara and Jessy sitting on the counter smiling like fools, waving at me. Sherri, Todd and Reilly are all standing in a row. They're all here, really here! But where's Laden?

Reilly steps forward does a slow blink and looks directly in the eyes of Mr. Stratler. In an instant, he backs up from my bedside and stops moving, like he's frozen. His men start to walk towards Reilly but also freeze. All of their eyes get big and shift from side to side.

"Are you preventing me from moving? You must be Reilly. I know all about you and your ability. Do you know who I am? You'd better release me immediately young man." Mr. Stratler is very angry and staring straight at Reilly. He is very intimidating but Reilly doesn't even flinch.

Sherri comes skipping past Reilly and stops directly in front of Mr. Stratler. She is as close to his face as she can get. "Do you know who we are? We're the kids who are going to stop you from taking our friend." She puts her hand on his arm. "This won't hurt a bit and when I'm done, I'll know everything that you know."

"Remove your hand young lady. You kids are all gifted because of me. It's all due to my research and my understanding of the human brain. I made you what you are today." Mr. Stratler pauses for a moment and softens his tone in his voice once he realizes that his threatening tone isn't getting him anywhere. "All of you could be very beneficial to your country. If you come with me, you will live out the rest of your lives with riches. You will never want for anything ever again. We are not here to hurt any of you." Mr. Stratler is trying to win us over. I don't trust him and I don't think my friends do either.

Tara walks over to me, holds my hand and brushes the hair off my face. "We've come to get you. You must have known that we'd never leave you."

Sherri takes her hand off of Mr. Stratler. "He's not the big shot money guy supporting this whole production, but he's responsible for a lot of it. He doesn't know who the head people are who ordered this. Doc Turner, this man here is the one who threatened your family." She moves on to read the other men. Sherri points her finger right at Mr. Stratler's nose. "You are in big trouble now mister!"

Doc Turner shakes his head. "Yes, I am well aware of that. I suppose I can tell you the whole story now. He threatened to take my wife and daughters and sell them overseas. At the time, my girls were only three and five years old. He said that I would never see them again but that my wife would be forced to watch our daughters go through hell every day. He said that they would wish for death."

Todd walks over to the glass wall separating Mabel Whitson's room and my room and points into the pitch black room where Mabel is probably unconscious. "She's lying in that bed unable to live her life because of you. That sweet girl can't do anything because of your actions. You ordered her to be drugged up so much that she can't even talk. Seriously, do you believe that you aren't hurting anyone? I'm sorry, but we can't trust you."

Todd struts over to Mr. Stratler. The man in the suit, a minute ago looking so in control, is now starting to cry.

Todd starts laughing. "I'm making you feel dread. The kind of dread that Mabel has most likely been feeling every single day that she's been in that bed. All I have to do is will that emotion on you, and voila, here you are, crying like a little girl who lost her puppy. I'm not even really trying, so how about I click it up a notch and fill you with despair? Horrible feeling isn't it?"

"Am I too late for the party?" The sweet, familiar sound of Laden's voice fills the room. He sounds chipper. He weaves his way through the frozen still men to get to my side. "I was helping a patient. I am here my love. He leans down and kisses my lips.

I can't believe that he left me here alone. Because of that, these men almost took me away. Where was he? Who was so important that he had to stay away from me?

Doc Turner and Nurse Karen stare at Laden and I. Doc steps forward to Laden. "Laden? Openly fraternizing with the patients is seriously frowned upon. You should have kept it secretly to yourselves. Do you love her?"

"Yes, I love Laura." Laden's eyes are filled with love, no fear, just pure love as he gazes into my eyes. "And I'm going to protect her from any experiments or people that might cause her even the slightest problem."

The lights flicker on and off, on and off. The men in the suits fall to the ground holding their heads in obvious agony. Blood streams from their eyes, noses and ears. Their cries of pain are muffled from the gurgling of blood that is now slowly drowning their lungs.

Todd yells to Reilly, "Stop! You're going to kill them. We don't want them dead, we want them in jail."

Reilly looks at Todd with his eyes huge, "Dude, I'm not doing that, I thought you were."

"No, I am." The shadow of a tiny, frail girl is standing at the door. She is wobbling, having a hard time holding her weight on her legs, even though she can't possibly weigh more than ninety pounds.

Laden says, "I was helping that patient." Suddenly, I totally forgive him. Is it possible that I can love him even more than I did before?

"Mabel?!" Reilly runs through the maze of bodies that are now writhing in pain on the floor. Seeing Mabel made him completely forget about his hold on the men, releasing them instantly. No matter, they're in too much pain to hurt anyone.

Reilly scoops Mabel up and wraps his arms around her, lifting her from her feet and spinning her around in a complete circle. Tears of happiness are spilling from his eyes.

Mabel wraps her arms around him and squeezes as best she can. "I waited for you. I knew you'd come back one day. I never gave up hope."

Reilly, so obviously elated says, "I didn't know you were here. They lied to us. But I'm here now, baby. I came as soon as I could."

Mabel pulls herself from his grasp and holds his face. "I know. We're together now, forever. But first, I have something to take care of." She kisses Reilly's lips tenderly then she turns back towards the room full of people. "Reilly, you'd better gather our friends and leave. I'll clean up the garbage. Karen, you've been good to me, you can go with them. Doc, you can leave too but you have a lot to answer for."

Reilly, Todd, Tara, Jessy and Sherri walk out the door. There's no need to sneak out under the veil of time freeze like on their way in.

Laden scoops me up in his arms and Nurse Karen unhooks my IV, lays the bag on me and the three of us exit the room. Doc Turner is the last to leave. Mr. Stratler and the men he brought with him are left to endure the wrath of Mabel Whitson.

With no one touching it, the door lightning fast slams shut and the room fills with grey fog. I try to see through it but I can't. Gut wrenching screams of men being tortured echo down the corridor. Red liquid splatters on the glass walls. It looks like blood.

Reilly stops then waves for us to continue on without him. "I'm not leaving Mabel again... ever. We'll catch up with you later."

We round the corner and leave through the door that Todd is holding open for everyone. Nurse Karen and Doc Turner stay at the nurses' station and tell us to go. The Restricted area's door shuts, sealing with a click.

CHAPTER

TWENTY-FIVE

The sun leaks in from the gaps in the drapes. I open my eyes to what looks to be a bright sunny day. I roll over and slide my arm over Laden's soft, bare chest. He puts his finger under my chin and lifts my face up to look at his.

"Good morning love." Laden kisses me softly.

"Good morning. How long have you been laying here awake?" I adore waking to his gentle face.

"All night... I didn't want to sleep. I was afraid I'd wake up and you would be gone. I didn't want to miss a second of how great it feels to have your warm, naked body pressed against mine. I just needed to hold you while you slept. You are so beautiful. Promise me that you'll always come back to me." Laden is so angelic when he speaks, so loving.

"When I was having my last vision, I got lost in the darkness and couldn't find my way back. The thing that scared me the most wasn't that I'd be stuck there forever, it was thinking that I would never see you again. You were my reason for not giving up. So you promise you'll always be here for me to come back to."

We seal our promises with a long kiss.

Tap, tap on the door. It must be 7:00...

COLOURS IN BLACKNESS
SERIES

Book #1   Book #2   Book #3
A New Life   Reprieve   Desolation

More to come

In Book #2 - Repreive

CHAPTER

ONE

A staff member comes around and taps on our doors right around 7am to make sure that we're awake for classes. It's kind of like a backup alarm clock. We live in a hospital/school for special kids. Special, meaning that we have unusual and powerful mental abilities.

All of us kids at this school have a special bond that will never be broken. We were all experimented on as babies by our pediatrician. His family was being threatened so he did as they said. He is still our doctor because he's regretful of his actions. We keep him around for his knowledge base and because we've grown to love him. It's a long story...

Tara must have shut her alarm off, fell back asleep and didn't hear the 'tap tap' on her door from the staff member this morning. She woke up when I came knocking at her door to collect her for breakfast. She usually comes to my door just before I open it. At the very least, we meet up in the hallway. Our rooms are right across the hall from each other.

Amazingly, Tara only takes ten minutes to get herself dressed and ready to go. She is definitely quicker than I am. It takes me ten minutes just to brush the tangles out of my long hair.

I pick up her backpack and hand it to her just after she shoves her feet into the suede boots that she loves so much. We rush out her door and sprint down to the mess hall for breakfast.

Human Behavioral Studies is exactly how it sounds. To put it simply is to say that it's very close to a psychology course. Most of the time, this class is totally captivating and usually has some level of intrigue, but not today. It's so boring that my eyes keep shutting on me.

I slept well last night so I don't know why I'm nodding off. Tara and Jessy keep tapping me to keep me awake but it's not working. I keep drifting. My eyes are so heavy. I just can't seem to fight it.

Blackness engulfs me then beautiful colours swirl in, overtaking the black. Wait! How can I be starting a vision if I'm not asleep or in deep concentration mode? I'm sitting in the middle of a classroom.

There wasn't any warning this time and no severe migraine pain, not even a headache. I didn't pass out on the floor either. At least I don't think I did. I'm not afraid I just don't understand.

A bubble starts to form in the middle of all the colours and I am being drawn towards it. I'm being pulled or maybe it's more like being pushed through the colours, slowly.

I hate this part, the waiting to arrive so I can get the full on view of what is to come. Will it be a good thing or full out terror? The latter is becoming the norm for me.

The bubble is growing bigger, coming closer and the scene inside of it is becoming clearer and clearer.

I see a version of me standing in a corridor, not moving, just standing still. Tara and Mabel are there with me. Both of them are talking to me, sort of yelling, panicking. Tara is patting my shoulder. Mabel is holding my hand trying to pull me. They look frantic like they need the frozen me to keep walking or something.

Suddenly Tara jumps behind this other me and Mabel spins around facing the way they were just coming from as if she's fearing something, or someone...